McAndrew's Stand

Jenny McAndrew and her two sons live in the valley known as McAndrew's Pass. When they hear the new Rocky Mountains Railroad Company has plans to lay a line through the valley and their farm, they are devastated that their simple life will be destroyed.

Clarence Harper, the ruthless boss of the railroad company, is not a man to brook opposition and will not leave without putting up a fight. In the McAndrews he finds one family that will not be bullied and battered into submission.

McAndrew's Stand

Bill Cartright

A Black Horse Western

ROBERT HALE · LONDON

ISBN 978-0-7198-1730-4

Robert Hale Limited
Clerkenwell House
Clerkenwell Green
London EC1R 0HT

www.halebooks.com

Typeset by
Derek Doyle & Associates, Shaw Heath
Printed and bound in Great Britain by
CPI Antony Rowe, Chippenham and Eastbourne

CHAPTER 1

It was a bright, clear afternoon in the early fall of 1866. Jenny McAndrew stood on the porch of her house looking out over the rich, fertile fields of the farm which she loved so dearly. The scene was one of utter tranquillity. The 150 acres of the McAndrews' spread stretched along the floor of the valley, hemmed in along two sides by the towering, rocky cliffs of the Sweetwater Mountains. The road between Fort Benton and Sawyer's Crossing bisected the farm and from her vantage point, Mrs McAndrew could see it running west, like a ribbon laid over the patchwork counterpane of the fields.

Although she wasn't one to put such thoughts into words, Jenny McAndrew was overwhelmed with a sudden feeling of contentment, tinged of course with sadness that her husband would never again share her pleasure at the view across McAndrew's Pass. It had been a shade over three years now since the news had reached her of Bob's death during the siege of

Vicksburg and although she had her two strong sons to rely upon, and they were a great comfort to her, the loss of her husband was a painful wound which would never entirely be healed.

There was one slight and, she hoped, insignificant, cloud on the horizon now and that was a letter which had been delivered that very day by a messenger from a business concern of which she had never heard, namely the Rocky Mountains Railroad Company. The rider, who had arrived half an hour earlier, had been polite and respectful, asking Mrs McAndrew if it would be possible for his boss to call on her at eight that evening, to discuss a matter which would be to their mutual advantage, as he put it. She fished the crumpled letter from her apron pocket, where she had stuffed it, smoothed it out and read it again. It was written on expensive, water-marked paper and the printed heading looked most impressive. The writer asked if he *might beg the favour of a few words with you this evening at eight, upon a matter which will be to our mutual advantage.* He signed himself Clarence Harper, Managing Director.

Tom, her eldest son and, at nineteen years of age, the spit image of his father in his younger days, came out of the barn where he had been working. Jenny called him over and handed him the letter, saying, 'What do you make to this here?'

'This what that fellow came by for to give you?'

'Yes, that's right.'

Tom McAndrew studied the letter carefully. He was no great scholar and it took him some time to make out every word. When he had finished, he handed it back to his mother and said, 'Don't you trust him, Ma.'

'How's that?'

'I'm telling you, any man who talks of "begging the favour" like that is too flowery and highfalutin' to be givin' an honest account of hisself. He's buttering you up and hoping to cheat you in some wise.'

'Lord a' mercy,' said Jenny McAndrew, 'If you don't sound just exactly like your father, God rest his soul! He would've said the self-same thing. I already thought so myself, but wanted your view to confirm it, if you know what I mean.'

'So what'll you do, Ma?'

'Well, I guess we'll let this Clarence Harper come here tonight and make his pitch. Least hear what he has to say.'

It was the age of the railroad; there had been nothing like it since the tulip mania, which had gripped Holland in the seventeenth century. Fortunes were being made, and lost, every day. Railroad shares could triple in value in a day or become worthless overnight. Some shrewd and unscrupulous businessmen had discovered that there was money to be made from railroads, even if they were never completed. What with government loans, land grants, subsidies, contracts for materials

7

which could be inflated, the rigging of the price of shares, wage bills which often bore no relation to the actual number of men being employed, and a hundred other tricks, the directors of the companies building the railroads grew rich on graft and corruption. In a number of cases, the companies collapsed after only a mile or two of track had been laid. Those who had invested their life savings in such enterprises were ruined, but the men who ran the businesses which failed in this way always seemed to end up in profit. One of this breed was Clarence Harper. The McAndrews had been very shrewd in spotting Harper as a crook, based solely upon the short letter he had written. A number of people who were far better educated and had a much wider experience of the world than Tom McAndrew and his mother, still hadn't seen Clarence Harper for what he was, even after a year or two's personal acquaintance with the man.

In 1862, Harper had been a member of the small group of financiers whose dream had been the creation of America's first transcontinental railroad, which would run from California to the east coast. The war was at its height and the Second Battle of Bull Run had just been fought and yet there were already those who were planning for the glorious future of a nation at peace; a country which would be covered from east to west in endless, gleaming railroad tracks which would cover the United States like a steel spider's web. The ground-breaking ceremony for the beginning of this project, the line which became known as the Union Pacific, took place at Omaha in December 1863. The principal speaker described the transcontinental railroad line as 'the grandest enterprise under God'.

Clarence Harper and one or two others involved in the construction of the Union Pacific soon realized that there was far more money to be made from *building* a railroad than there was from actually *running* or even completing one. They created a phantom company called Credit Mobilier, which was supposedly being paid to carry out much of the work on the new railroad. Since Credit Mobilier was in reality owned by Harper and his friends, they were, in effect, paying themselves from the money they had been receiving in loans from Washington.

The more far-sighted of these swindlers, Harper included, took their profits and got out before the scandal erupted and questions began to be asked in Congress about the bottomless pit of taxpayers' money that was the Union Pacific Railroad. Harper was mixed up in one or two similar confidence tricks until he had the inspiration of raising the money for, and building, his own railroad line. This would supposedly run north west from Council Bluffs in Iowa, all the way to the Pacific coast, near the Canadian border. The line, linking up at a junction in Council Bluffs with the Union Pacific, was to be called the

Rocky Mountains Railroad. It was not until Harper had begun this immense undertaking that he discovered that he might have bitten off more than he was comfortably able to swallow.

Others at about this time had a similar idea of constructing a line in roughly the same direction as the Rocky Mountains Railroad. While these rivals fiddled around with surveyors and lawyers, Clarence Harper began work at once, sinking every cent he owned into the enterprise. If it came off, he would be the wealthiest man in the whole of the United States; if it failed, he would be ruined. It was not until work had been underway for six months that it dawned on Harper that this time he would actually have to complete the damned project before he was able to recoup any profit. After the Credit Mobilier débâcle, newspapers were watching closely the progress of new long-distance railroad lines. Clarence Harper's name had already been mentioned in connection with Credit Mobilier and, if he tried to cream off money and vanish from the scene of his latest project, it would surely become a police matter. There was nothing for it but to forge ahead and finish what he had begun.

By paring expenditure to the very bone, hiring Chinese coolies at half the rate that he would have to pay white workers and neglecting many basic safety precautions, Harper was still on target to become an enormously rich man, but only if and when his line reached the coast. He drove on, sometimes across land belonging to others, violating treaties with the Indians, and generally riding roughshod over any objections. By a combination of bribery, leavened with the judicious use of violence when nothing else would serve, the Rocky Mountains Railroad was, astonishingly, ahead of schedule as it passed through Montana towards the Rockies. It was then that Harper's plans hit the metaphorical buffers, as he explained that evening to Mrs McAndrew and her sons.

'I'm going to level with you, Mrs McAndrew,' announced Harper, sincerity radiating from his face, 'That's my nature, I'm afraid. Folk tell me that I'm just too open and honest for my own good and that it'll be my downfall one fine day.'

'What a mercy that we are going to be honest with each other, Mr Harper,' said Jenny McAndrew, 'It should make our dealings easier.'

'Yes indeed,' replied Harper, who might have been one of the shrewdest businessmen in the country but was apparently oblivious to sarcasm and irony. 'Here's how matters stand. The railroad is coming. There's no getting away from it for any of us. One day, every small village will be within reach of a railroad depot and nobody will bother with horses any more. That being so, the smart folk, men of the world like me and women who look ahead, like you, do our best to see how to work this coming situation

11

to our own advantage.'

Out of the corner of her eye, Jenny was uneasily aware that her sons were shifting in their seats as though they had opinions to express on the subject. She had impressed upon the boys most forcibly, that they were to leave the talking to her, at least until they found out what it was that this smooth-talking fellow was after.

Clarence Harper continued, 'Let me show you this map.' He unfolded a large-scale map across the table, upon which was marked in red the projected route of the Rocky Mountains Railroad line. Jenny saw, to her amazement and indignation, that the blood-red streak passed clean through the valley where she lived. Indeed, it ran straight through the very house in which they were sitting, as far as she could make out. For a few seconds, she was unable to speak. It felt as though she had received a blow to her stomach which had knocked the breath from her body. Then she said slowly, 'Do my eyes deceive me, or is this line of yours supposed to be passing through my home? I only ask, because in such a case, it seems to me that this concerns me and my family.'

Without saying a word, her sons, 19-year-old Tom and 17-year-old Jack, stood up from the table and then moved round behind their mother, looking over her shoulder at the map. Tom drew in breath sharply when he saw the path of the projected railroad line and he looked up, glaring balefully at

Clarence Harper.

'Let me get this clear, Mr Harper,' said Mrs McAndrew, 'You started building your railroad, aiming all along to take it across my land and only now are you seeking my permission. Is that how the case stands?'

Harper laughed. 'Put like that, I freely admit, it sounds a little rich, don't it? But before you get all het up, let me explain a little.'

'I'm not going to get het up; you may rest easy on that point.'

'How it was, is that I sent a fellow this way before drawing up my plans. He said that this valley was the only route through the Sweetwater Mountains and that there was a lot of rough pasture along by the cliffs, which would be perfect for laying our tracks. We can't go along the south side of the valley, you see, because the ground there is mighty soggy, on account of the little stream running along there.'

'As far as it goes,' admitted Mrs McAndrew thoughtfully, 'that's all true. The only thing is, I happen to own that pasture you talk of and it's not for sale.'

'This valley of yours, it runs for what, eight miles through the mountains?'

'That's correct.'

'It's right narrow too, no more than a mile wide at most?'

'Closer to half a mile here. With sheer cliffs along

13

the sides for the whole length of it.'

Not at all put off by Mrs McAndrew's anything but encouraging attitude, Clarence Harper smiled broadly, shaking his head. 'You know, when first I saw the name of this valley, McAndrew's Pass, it never once occurred to me that there would really be anybody called McAndrew living here. Thought it was just the name of some explorer or other from long ago.'

'So it was. It was my husband's grandfather who found this valley over sixty years ago. He set up here when it was just wild country all around. After he'd lived here for twelve years, he filed a claim and the family have lived here ever since.'

'All we need, Mrs McAndrew, is a narrow strip of land from one end of your valley to the other. You don't own the land further on, towards Fort Benton, do you?'

'Not a bit of it. Just the hundred and fifty acres here.'

'Problem is, ma'am, anything other than going through this pass, well, it would mean a detour of nearly two hundred miles north or south to get round these mountains. They're too high to go over, too big to go through. Your valley is the only way for the line to make it through from Sawyer's Crossing, which we're approaching, to Fort Benton. We have to go through here.'

'That's no affair of mine,' said Mrs McAndrew. 'I

didn't tell you to come this way with your locomotives.'

Harper continued as though she had not spoken. 'We can't route the line along the road running through here, on account of it's a right of way. There'd be no end of legal difficulties. The other side of this valley has a stream running along it, which makes the ground too boggy. That leaves only this land alongside these cliffs.'

'Well, Mr Harper,' said Jenny politely, 'I'm sorry not to oblige, but you see that would mean having railroad locomotives running about six feet from our windows and I don't somehow take to the notion.'

The Managing Director of the Rocky Mountains Railroad Company smiled again and said reassuringly, 'Oh, my company would compensate you adequately for the loss of amenity.'

'We're not selling any of our land and there's an end to it.'

Harper was about to speak again, but Tom McAndrew cut in, saying quietly, 'When my ma says something, she generally means it. You best listen to what she's a' tellin' you now.'

Not in the least out of countenance, Harper got to his feet and said cheerfully, 'Well, I won't take up any more of your time, ma'am. Think over what I've said, and then we'll discuss terms in a week or so.'

With perfect affability, Jenny McAndrew also rose and shook hands with her visitor. Harper bowed

15

gracefully and, before taking his leave, turned to the two boys. Jack and Tom were standing behind their mother, both looking coldly at the man from the railroad, who remarked, 'I have seldom seen such pleasant and well-mannered young fellows. Goodbye, the two of you. It has been a pleasure visiting in such a nice home.'

Long ago, Clarence Harper had learned not to let other people know what he was thinking. In the present instance, this was just as well, because what he had been thinking in the McAndrews' house was how much he would have relished the opportunity of throwing Mrs Jennifer McAndrew to the floor and ravishing her. Still, that wasn't business. As he rode back to Sawyer's Crossing, Harper turned over in his mind one or two schemes for persuading the stubborn jackasses living in the little valley that their best interests lay in co-operating with the railroad company.

What Harper hadn't seen fit to mention during his visit was that it was desperately urgent that there be not the slightest delay in pushing the line through to Fort Benton. Although he had begun his line to the north Pacific coast before anybody else, there were now two contenders for being the first to reach that spot he was heading for – the new port on the Pacific, just south of the Canadian border. Like him, those building the lines had the newly established township called Seattle, marked down as a place likely to be prosperous and important in the years to come. The other lines had begun further north than his own: one from Grand Forks and the other from Minneapolis. The Great Northern and the North Pacific would both be passing north of the Sweetwater Mountains. His only advantage was that he would be driving straight through them and was already ahead of the others going in the same direction. If he had to start a detour, then his company might even run out of money and work come to a halt. That would be the end of him; he would be a penniless bankrupt.

He cursed himself for a fool. Many of the farmers in out-of-the-way places hadn't proved up on their land and were, in effect, squatters. Such people were in no good position to object if a railroad company chose to run its track through a corner of their land. The case was different though with the McAndrews. Somehow, the damned clown whom Harper had engaged to scout out the area had overlooked the fact that the McAndrews had solid, legal title to all the land from one side of that pass to the other. That wasn't how it was with the other families in the valley. For the sake of good will, he might throw them a few dollars for the use of the pasture running along the side of the mountain, but they had no legal right to the land. Before he could make it there though, he'd have to reach an accommodation with Mrs McAndrew and her boys. He'd double check with his tame lawyer that there was no way of cheating them out of the land, otherwise things might get a little lively up at that little farm.

It took Harper over two hours to ride back to Sawyer's Crossing and it was nearly midnight before he saw the lights of the town twinkling ahead of him.

The arrival in a small town of a crew building a railroad was seldom an unalloyed blessing. The chief beneficiaries tended to be the proprietors of cathouses and saloons. There was certainly money being thrown around, but many citizens thought that the problems caused by hundreds of navigators descending upon a quiet town were greater than the money thus generated. Harper went to the Tanglefoot, which was where his most reliable men had been drinking. Although it was only Tuesday, the saloon was more crowded than it would have been on a normal Saturday night. As a rule, coolies would have a long wait at the bar before realizing that they were not welcome at the Tanglefoot, but the owner wasn't inclined to turn away so much trade and for once he had relaxed all the usual rules. Black and white, Mexican and Chinese all rubbed shoulders together in the Tanglefoot that night.

It wasn't Clarence Harper's custom to go hunting out those with whom he wished to speak. It was more dignified and befitting a man of his stature, he thought, to wait for others to come to him. He didn't have to wait long before one of his men nudged the

18

other and drew attention to the fact that the boss was standing just inside the batwing doors, evidently wishing to speak to somebody. The two fellows who approached Harper now had an ill-defined but vital role in the company. They were the ones who fixed the more serious difficulties that cropped up from time to time: Don Rutledge was nominally 'Business Manager' and Abe Goldman dealt with legal matters. Goldman had not been involved with Harper as long as Rutledge had. He was a lawyer who had been disbarred and found that working for the Rocky Mountains Railroad might be the way back into professional life.

Goldman said, 'Everything go all right up at that McAndrew's Pass place, boss?' Harper liked to be addressed as 'boss' and Goldman was sycophantic enough to play up to this at every opportunity.

'Not so you'd notice,' replied Harper sourly. 'I think there's going to be some work for the pair of you up that way.'

'What sort o' work?' asked Rutledge. 'Hard man to deal with?'

Clarence Harper snorted. 'Not a bit of it. Woman and two snot-nosed boys. Soft as butter. You might even be able to have a little fun with the mother, if you can handle the thing well and clear the way for us to move through.'

CHAPTER 2

The 150 acres of the McAndrews' farm should, theoretically at least, have been more than sufficient to provide the three people living there with everything they needed to flourish. The only problem was that when Bob McAndrew had gone off to war in 1861, heeding Mr Lincoln's call for volunteers after the shelling of Fort Sumter, one of his sons had been fourteen and the other twelve. It would have needed some years of training before they would have been able to run the place effectively. As it was, they and their mother did the best they could, but the best that they could manage was to grub out a living and somehow fend off starvation. Some of their neighbours along the valley towards Fort Benton did better and others worse. But the main thing was that the straggling line of settlements along the eight-mile-long strip of land known as McAndrews's Pass were free and beholden to nobody. They were a tough and independent body of men and women who asked only to be left in peace.

At seventeen, Jack McAndrew was not quite fully grown and therefore not as useful as his brother Tom when it came to ploughing a field or chopping wood. He had a special talent though which was his almost uncanny facility with firearms. Most mornings, Jack went out with his scattergun looking for meat for the pot. Birds, jack-rabbits nor the occasional deer stood any chance at all when the young lad carrying his father's old fowling piece came into sight. That morning had been a profitable one and Jack had bagged a fawn, which he carried draped over his shoulders as though he were a born mountain man.

As Jack picked his way down the path from the mountains and back to his home, he saw two men riding along the road from Sawyer's Crossing. Tom had gone off for the day and Jack felt that right now, he was the man of the family which meant that he was responsible for keeping an eye on what went on round the farm. When the two riders halted and dismounted, he accordingly speeded up his pace and began hurrying down the slope in case his mother had need of him.

The road to Fort Benton ran through the McAndrews' farm dividing it roughly in half. That day, two men had reined in their horses, having come down the road from Sawyer's Crossing and, after dismounting, were now picking their way delicately

21

across the field to where Jenny McAndrew was harvesting roots. One of the men was Clarence Harper, who greeted the woman cheerfully. 'Good day to you, Mrs McAndrew,' he said. 'You have a fine day for your agricultural pursuits.'

'I have, if we're not delayed overmuch,' she said pointedly.

Harper laughed and said, 'I won't keep you but a few moments. I was wondering if you had given any thought to what we discussed last week?'

'Mr Harper,' said Jenny McAndrew patiently, 'You have your work and I have mine. Yours is, as I understand it, to build a railroad line. I have no interest in stopping you and wish you well with the project. It has nothing to do with me. My business is farming and I am currently engaged in harvesting, which I am unable to undertake while standing here and gossiping with you. None of my land is for sale and there's an end to it.'

'I'm sorry to hear you take that line,' said Harper. He shrugged, an expression of regret on his face. 'I had you pegged for a woman who wasn't stuck in the old ways, somebody who welcomed the new world we're seeing. Seems as I was mistaken.' He turned away, apparently saddened at such short-sighted obstinacy. As he did so, Harper raised one eyebrow in an almost imperceptible signal to the man standing beside him. This fellow then addressed the woman in the following way.

'I thought you'd'a had more sense, ma'am. My boss here is offering you a right good price for the little bit o' land we want and you just throw his generosity back in his face.'

'Who might you be?' asked Mrs McAndrew quietly.

'I'm the business manager of the Rocky Mountains Railroad and my job is to deal with any stubborn mules as is holding things up. Now we can do this the easy way, where you sell to us peaceable like, or we can do it the hard way, when folk might get hurt. I wouldn't want to go down that path, not if I had children.' Don Rutledge stepped closer to Mrs McAndrew until he was only two feet from her. She stepped back instinctively, a look of fear on her face.

The two men had been so intent on menacing a woman, that they had not been aware of the young man approaching stealthily from behind. The first they knew of the matter was the sharp, metallic click of a gun being cocked. They turned to see boy of about seventeen or eighteen years of age, drawing down on them with a double-barrelled scattergun.

'Say now,' said Harper uneasily, 'You best lower that weapon, son. We don't want anybody getting hurt here.'

'Tell that fellow to step away from my ma,' said Jack McAndrew evenly. 'And then tell him to come stand alongside you.' When there was no immediate reaction, the boy said, 'I tell you now, I've a taken first pull on the trigger. If'n I so much as sneeze or fart, I'm apt to blow you to hell.'

'Do as he says,' Harper told Don Rutledge. 'Just let Mrs McAndrew be and come over next to me.'

Neither Clarence Harper nor his 'business manager' were carrying iron, as they preferred in their day-to-day work to appear in the character of respectable businessmen. Rutledge did as his boss had bid him, but he was glaring evilly at the youth and it was plain that he was ready and willing to tackle the boy if an opportunity presented itself to do so. Realizing this, Jack McAndrew said, 'Holding this gun at my shoulder like this is awkward. I sure hope I don't get any sudden shocks or jerks, for any mistake I make now ain't likely to be put right in this world.'

Harper gave Don Rutledge a warning look, as if to tell him not to take any chances. Then he said, 'What do you want us to do, son? Seems like you hold all the cards here.'

'We're a' goin' to walk real slow back to the road, where you left your horses. Then the two of you can saddle up and head back the way you come.'

'Sure thing,' said Harper pleasantly, 'Nobody wants to see any shooting, do they?'

'Depends if you do as I say,' said the young man. 'Don't think I'd hesitate to pull this trigger if I'm pushed to it.'

'Best make sure then that we all take it easy,' said Harper. 'That sounds like it suits all parties.'

Slowly, the three of them made their way across the field and back to the road where the two horses were patiently waiting. Every step of the way, Jack McAndrew kept the whole of his attention focused upon the two men walking in front of him. Despite his tough words, he doubted his ability to shoot a living person down and was glad to see that he probably wasn't about to be put to the test. It was enough that those men believed that he would do so.

When they got to the road, Jack stopped, keeping his scattergun still trained upon the railroad man and his employee. He said quietly and reasonably, 'My mother has told you she's not sellin' and that's all there is to know. Don't either of you come back here.' The two men mounted up and left without bidding Jack any sort of farewell.

When Tom got back, later that same afternoon, it was all that his mother could do to stop him from riding straight off to Sawyer's Crossing and shooting Clarence Harper and anybody associated with him. 'Tom,' she told him urgently, 'there's no harm been done. They didn't lay a finger on me, and Jack here, he sent them on their way. It's finished.'

Tom looked as though he was heeding her words and Jenny was pleased to think that she had calmed things down, when her younger son chipped in, saying, 'It ain't over, not by a long sight.'

'Hush your mouth,' his mother told him sharply, 'I said it's over and over it is.'

25

'Don't like to contradict you, Ma,' said Jack softly, ' 'Course it ain't over yet. Those men'll be back. We got something they just can't do without.'

'Jack's right,' said his brother. 'Maybe I shouldn't go charging down to Sawyer's Crossing after those fellows, but we can't forget 'em.'

'All right,' said Jenny, 'What do you boys say we should do?'

There was a pause, while Tom and Jack mulled over the question. Then Tom said, 'First off is we need to make sure that this place is secure and nobody can get in and take us by surprise. . . .'

When Ebeneezer McAndrew settled in the gap between the Sweetwater Mountains in 1805, the area was completely wild and from all that he was able to make out, he was the first white man that many of the Indians living around those parts had ever set eyes upon. Nobody ever knew what it was that had drawn Ebeneezer McAndrew to that spot, nor why, having arrived there with his young bride, he should have thought it a good location to settle. But settle he did, and it was right there, in the place known later as McAndrew's Pass, that the pioneer built his house. That first dwelling-house was a miserable, poky affair, scarcely larger than a pig pen. Over the succeeding years though, McAndrew enlarged and fortified his home.

Most of the Indians in that part of what would one day become Montana, were more or less indifferent to the presence of a white man and woman living near them. Those were the days before it became plain that there was not room in the land for both the red and white man. Some Indians though *did* object to seeing a stone-built house belonging to a white man being raised on their hunting grounds. A group of Lakota who later became known as the Hunkpapa, used to raid the fields which Ebeneezer had cleared and cultivated and also menace his house. His home became a fortified redoubt, with stout wooden shutters which could be drawn across the windows and firing ports in each external wall. In time, the Lakota accepted this lone settler and by the time his son, Tom and Jack's grandfather, grew to manhood, the McAndrews were as much a part of the landscape as their Indian neighbours.

All of which meant that if you had sought high and low around that part of Montana, you would have been hard pressed to find a more defensible position than the McAndrews' house. Once the doors were locked and the shutters down, it would have been no easy task to gain entry to the place; other than by the use of explosives.

In fact, it was by means of explosives that Clarence Harper's two main helpers in the Rocky Mountains Railroad Company proposed to solve what they saw as a bottleneck which was holding up their operations. Don Rutledge was fuming with anger after he and his boss had been turfed off the McAndrews' fields. Rutledge's chief selling point as Harper's right-hand man was his willingness to use violence against anybody who was opposed to the interests of their project. It was for this, rather than any intellectual ability that he was prized. If a problem arose which could not be smoothed over by negotiation, or a little crooked legal work, then it was to Don Rutledge that Harper turned. Being ordered about at gunpoint by a kid had wounded Rutledge's vanity and, he thought, lowered him in the estimation of the boss. He was determined to avenge the insult and also to regain what he saw as lost face.

Abe Goldman was a shifty, whey-faced individual who looked as though he wouldn't be a whole lot of use in a rough house. It was for his brains that Clarence Harper valued him. He was every bit as mean as Rutledge in his own way, but preferred to avoid using his boots and fists to get one over on those he came up against. He hadn't been a crony of Harper's for as long as Rutledge, but had risen fast in the boss's favour and Goldman had been secretly delighted to hear of the way in which Rutledge had been humiliated.

'What you going to do about that business up at McAndrew's Pass?' Goldman asked his supposed partner that evening, as they relaxed in the tent which they shared. Rutledge did not have the wits to realize that the other man was eager to supplant him and assume for himself the title of business manager.

He thought that Goldman was his friend.

'We're running out o' time,' said Rutledge. 'In a fortnight or so, we'll be at the pass and we'll need to have dealt with those bastards 'fore then.'

'So what d'you say we should do? The boss is getting a mite restless about it, thinks we ought to fix things.'

It had struck Goldman that his partner would most likely have some sort of scheme already in his head for fixing the problem of the McAndrews and he was anxious that he should appear to Harper to have been involved in clearing the way through the Sweetwaters. As long as the plan that Rutledge came up with didn't call for too much in the way of gunplay or fistfights, he thought that tagging along on the expedition might make him look like a man of action and not just the shyster lawyer that some took him to be.

Rutledge noted that Abe Goldman used the word 'we' and was strangely touched. He said, 'You comin' to help?'

'Surely. What have you in mind?'

While Harper's two men were mulling over their plans, the McAndrew brothers were also doing their best to figure out what would be wise. They went out to the barn on the pretext of working, but they really wanted to talk over what had happened without their mother hearing. This was less a question of being sly than a laudable desire not to worry a woman with what they both regarded as being the proper business of men. 'We need to make sure the house is safe at night,' said Jack. 'I mind those men are the sort as might think of sending somebody up here to do some mischief or other.'

His brother looked worried. Although he was not yet twenty, a good deal of the burden of running the farm had descended upon his shoulders following his father's departure to the war. It had been a lot for a boy of fourteen to be burdened with. His pa had only returned on furlough for the odd two or three weeks at a time and had advised his eldest son as best he was able, but Tom had still had to grow up very fast. He said to his brother, 'I mind that you're right, Jack. We'd best check the shutters and test the locks tonight. We need to make certain-sure that nobody can get into the house while we sleep and murder us in our beds.'

'That's the way of it, all right. But that's not the end of it. Those rogues'll be back, maybe a whole bunch of them. What we goin' to do then?' To this question, Tom McAndrew had no answer.

The scheme that Don Rutledge outlined to Goldman was simple, bloody and likely to prove devastatingly effective. The two of them had removed a ten pound keg of fine grain powder from the stores, along with a good long length of fuse. There was plenty of powder used for blasting rocks before laying the rails and it was unlikely that anybody would remark on the removal of ten pounds of the stuff. Clarence Harper expected things to be done which made life easier, but he didn't like to be given chapter and verse of the methods used. It suited him if he could honestly deny knowledge of what his subordinates had been up to on his behalf. Nobody would be gladder than Harper to see the McAndrew family removed, but if, on the other hand, things went wrong and the law caught Rutledge and Goldman, then he would certainly act shocked and pretend that he'd had no idea of the lengths to which his men might go.

From what he could make out, Abe Goldman wouldn't actually have to engage in any rough stuff, just accompany Rutledge and maybe fire a couple of times towards the house when they got there. The plan was, typically for Rutledge, perfectly straightforward. They would creep up on the farm at night when everybody would be in bed. Then they would bury the keg of powder at the base of a wall and set a fuse to it. There was an excellent chance that those in the house would be killed in the explosion, but if not, then they would be sure to come running out of the place and it should then be easy enough to pick them off with rifles. After that, the two of them would just mount up and ride back to Sawyer's Crossing. Nobody would be more surprised than they to hear that the whole family had been massacred in the night.

'You in?' asked Don Rutledge, when he had out-lined what he planned to do.

'I'm in,' Goldman had replied. He felt at the moment that he was starting to get an edge on the other man as far as Harper's view of them was concerned. Allowing the boss to be thrown off that farm at gunpoint hadn't done Rutledge any good as regards being seen as a tough fellow and Goldman was anxious to make it seem that he kept up now with whatever Rutledge was doing. The slow-witted fellow was likely to trip up soon and Goldman wanted to be there to take full advantage of the situation when this eventually happened.

Mrs McAndrew sensed that the boys had been talking privately about what was happening and before they went to bed that night, she spoke seriously to them. 'I know fine well that the two of you think you're grown men now and are taking care o' me. I'm grateful as you feel that way and more proud than you'll know. All the same, I lost your father, God rest him, to violence, and I don't want to be grieving again for one or other of you. I tell you plain, fond as I am of this place, I'd sooner give it up right this second than set here and run any risk to you two. You're more precious to me than any old farm.'

'We ain't a' goin' to be taking any chances, Ma,' Tom assured her. 'You make yourself easy. Me and Jack here are just keeping an eye out. We're not aimin' to fight, nor nothing of that sort.'

'Jack,' said his mother, 'you're keeping quiet. You mark what I said just now?'

'I heard you, Ma. Same like Tom here says, we're not wanting any fighting. We just want to make sure that no harm befalls you.'

Their mother looked at her sons in the flickering light from the candles. She said, 'You're good boys and a great comfort to me. Just recollect what I say and know that I'd sooner have the both of you alive and well than the fanciest farm in the country.' She looked at them fondly and then said, 'I'm bound for bed now. You boys coming up too?'

'We'll be up directly, Ma,' said Jack, 'Just want to talk over one or two things as need doing in the morning, then we'll be for our beds too.'

'Well then, goodnight.'

Tom and Jack wished their mother goodnight and then, as soon as they were certain that she was upstairs and safely out of earshot, they discussed what needed doing. 'What say,' said Tom quietly, 'that we take turn and turn about, hiding in the barn, watching the house and fields?'

'Sounds good. Who goes first?'

'Toss you. Loser takes first watch.' Tom ferreted about in his pocket and pulled out a dime. He spun this into the air, catching it neatly on his palm and then slapping it down on the back of his left hand, keeping the coin covered from view. 'Call!' he said.

'Heads.'

Tom lifted his right hand to reveal that it was indeed heads. He said to his brother, 'Get your head down and I'll call you to take over at about one.'

CHAPTER 3

The moon was full and unobscured by clouds, casting a light almost as bright as day upon the fields of the McAndrews' farm. The stout farmhouse stood on a little rise of land, a short distance from the cliffs of the Sweetwater Mountains. It was a tranquil scene. Don Rutledge and Abe Goldman reined in their horses and surveyed the land before them.

There were no lights in the house which, combined with the lateness of the hour, suggested that the inhabitants were likely to be sleeping. 'What do you think,' said Goldman, 'we should go ahead with this?'

'You bet. You ain't chicken, I suppose?'

'Not a bit of it. Say though, I was wondering, there's another five or six farms along this valley. We're not going to have to repeat the exercise with each and every one of 'em, are we?'

Don Rutledge gave a short bark, which was the

nearest he ever got to laughing. 'One'll do the trick. The rest'll soon fall into line. Once folk know that it's life and death, they'll be only too glad to sell a strip of land to the boss, you'll see. You gotta make an example of somebody first, so's the others get the idea.'

This all made perfect sense to Goldman, although he was not personally a violent man. He was quite happy to go along with the murder of an entire family if it would increase his standing with Clarence Harper. With luck, he thought, a little of the credit for this night's work might rub off on him and maybe people would begin seeing him too as a ruthless and determined man, rather than just a failed, two-bit lawyer on the make.

'You think that keg o' powder will be enough to finish them all off?' asked Goldman casually, as though blowing up houses were all in a day's work for him, 'It looks mighty small for the job.'

'It might not bring down the house entirely,' replied Rutledge, 'But it'll surely cause those inside who are still alive to come running out to see what the Sam Hill is going on! Then you and me'll just shoot 'em down. It'll be a regular turkey shoot!'

The thought of gunning down a woman and her sons like that did not appeal to Abe Goldman overmuch, but he guessed that all he would need to do would be to fire in their general direction. There was no need for him actually to hit anybody. He knew that Rutledge was a crack shot and would certainly be able to take out three people in a few seconds. All that Goldman felt that he needed to do was show willing.

The two of them tethered their horses on the picket fence which separated the road from the McAndrew fields and then made their way quietly towards the house. Both men were carrying rifles and would position themselves far enough from the house that they would not be in hazard from the explosion, but close enough to be able to kill those who would flee in terror once Rutledge's mine was sprung.

So far, everything was going precisely according to plan and Abe Goldman was hopeful that they would be able to kill the folk living here and then be on their way back to Sawyer's Crossing before anybody else had a chance to come up here to investigate. What neither he nor Rutledge knew, of course, was that Tom McAndrew had been observing the pair of them from the moment that they left the road and began making the way across the fields towards the house. Tom drew the Colt Navy from where it was tucked in his belt and cocked it. The pistol had been returned to them after Vicksberg, along with his father's other personal effects, and over the three years since then, he had practised enough to become a fair to middling shot with the weapon.

When they were twenty yards from the farmhouse,

Rutledge indicated to his companion that they should halt. He set the wooden keg that he was carrying on the ground and then pulled out the length of fuse which he inserted through the bung-hole. His original idea had been to dig a hole at the base of one of the walls of the house and then tamp down the charge properly, like he was undertaking a demolition, or blasting a rock face. It had occurred to him though that the sound of digging might alert the occupants of the building to their peril. He didn't want to be squatting there, scraping a hole in the earth and then find somebody sending a charge of buckshot through the top of his head. So now Rutledge had decided simply to place the keg against a wall and hope for the best. There would be enough explosive force to wreck the interior of the house and quite possibly injure or kill those within. It was when he had finished inserting the fuse and was about to stand up and take the powder over to the house, that Don Rutledge looked up and saw that a man with a pistol in his hand was watching him with great interest.

Abe Goldman had been so intent upon watching Rutledge prepare his bomb that he hadn't noticed somebody walking quietly up behind him. He saw the surprised look in Rutledge's eyes and realized that there was something behind him. He turned, to find a levelled pistol aiming right at his belly. The young man holding the gun said, 'Just let drop that

38

rifle. Right now or I swear to God I'll kill you.'

There was no percentage in being a tough guy and Goldman opened his fingers and let the rifle fall to the ground. The boy, for he was hardly old enough to be called a man, said, 'You down there on the ground. You stand up, real slow.'

If there was one thing that Don Rutledge detested above all else, it was being bossed about by somebody with a gun. He'd killed an officer in the Confederate Army for doing that very thing during the war and since then, nobody had managed to get the drop on him like this. He toyed with the notion of snatching up his rifle, but from the look of it, this youth knew what he was about and his piece was cocked. Rutledge thought that he would need to try another tack. He rose slowly to his feet and said, 'I see you think you got cause to take me on. Maybe you have an' maybe you've not. Tell you what though, anybody can be a big man with a gun in his hand. Specially when his enemy is unarmed.'

Appealing to the boy's sense of fair play and hinting at cowardice was about the only string in Don Rutledge's bow and he frankly didn't hold out much hope of success from the tactic. He certainly wouldn't have allowed himself to be buffaloed into surrendering the advantage that this young fellow had. Still, Tom McAndrew was only nineteen and a mite sensitive about being thought of as unable to meet an opponent on equal terms. The uncertainty showed in his face and Rutledge gambled everything on this one weak spot. He said, 'I'll warrant you wouldn't set aside that weapon of yours and face me man to man, just the two of us with our fists. Then we'd see a thing or two.'

This schoolyard talk struck a chord in Tom McAndrew's young heart and, irrational as it was, he felt suddenly ashamed of the advantage he held over the older man, by virtue of holding the pistol. He also resented the suggestion that he was afraid to meet this bully man to man, in a straight contest of physical prowess. Incredible to relate, he said, 'You want that we two should set to together? Without weapons?'

Don Rutledge could scarcely believe his luck. Although this was what he'd been pushing the boy for, he had not really dared hope that it would work.

'I mind you fellows are from that railroad man,' said Tom, 'and I'll show you what I think of you and your boss.' He bent down, never once taking his eyes from the other men and put his pistol down carefully on the ground. Then he made a rush at Rutledge, driving him back. It had been Rutledge's intention to pick up his rifle and shoot the boy, if once he could persuade him to put down his own weapon, but he hadn't expected to be attacked like this at once. The two of them wrestled, the boy clamping his arms around the older man in a fierce bear hug. Don Rutledge was no weakling, but he felt at once the lithe, muscular strength in those arms and hoped that he would be able to prevail against the youngster.

The truth was that Tom McAndrew was used to working a twelve-hour day around the farm and he neither drank nor smoked. He was a good fifteen years younger than Rutledge, who was, in any case, a little flabby and out of condition, relying as he did these days on firearms, rather than his physical force. Rutledge stamped down hard on the youngster's foot and then followed this up with a sharp punch in the ribs. Being so close to his target meant that he wasn't able to swing his fist all that hard, but the blow achieved the effect for which he hoped, in that it caused Tom to release his hold.

The two men circled warily around each other, both looking for an opening. There was not the least doubt which of them had the greatest motivation in this encounter. The younger man was fighting on his home ground for what he saw as the good of his family, whereas Rutledge was essentially motivated only by money and self-interest. Then again, McAndrew was a decent young fellow and was fighting fair. He certainly didn't know any of the dirty tricks which were second nature to Rutledge. However, he didn't need any of those dodges, because he swung a knotty fist into the side of Rutledge's jaw, which sent the other man sprawling to the ground. As he attempted to rise, young

McAndrew swung his boot into Rutledge's ribs, sending him flying.

Although he hadn't really planned to take a very active role in the operation, it was becoming increasingly plain to Goldman that his partner was not really up to the job of handling this savage young man. Accordingly he picked up the rifle that he had thrown down, cocked the hammer and then, without even raising it to his shoulder or taking more than the vaguest aim, he squeezed the trigger. The result of this haphazard operation surpassed the lawyer's wildest expectations. It had been a matter of sheer chance whether he hit anybody at all and, if so, if it would be Tom McAndrew or Don Rutledge. Fortune sometimes smiles on fools though and Goldman found to his astonishment that he had succeeded in shooting the younger of the two combatants in the back.

Tom stood up very straight, like a man with a bad backache who is stretching to relieve the pain, and then toppled forward, landing face down in front of the man he had just recently kicked. Rutledge got to his feet as somebody kindled a light in the house. Presumably the brief conversation earlier between Rutledge and the boy had disturbed one of those asleep in the farmhouse. Then a window was thrown up and a male voice called out, 'Throw up your hands or I'll fire!' No sooner had the warning been issued, than there was the hollow boom of a scattergun, which echoed to and fro between the rocky cliffs on either side of the little valley. Don Rutledge gave a cry of vexation and anger.

'Come on,' he yelled. 'We're better out of this.' He picked up his rifle and began sprinting back to where they'd left the horses. As they ran off, there was another shot.

It wasn't until the two men from the railroad were well on their way that Rutledge revealed that he'd been hit in the arm. 'Is it bad?' asked Goldman, having had very little experience of gunshot wounds.

'Bit o' buckshot, I reckon. Stings, but nothing serious. Happen you'll be able to help pick it out when we get back to town.'

A second after hearing the shot and then shouting out of the window at the men standing near his house, Jack McAndrew had seen his brother lying still in the dirt and had let fly with both barrels. Then he had thrown down his weapon and run downstairs to see if he could do anything for Tom. It was lucky for him that the two men had decided that they'd had enough, because Jack ran from the house heedless and unarmed. He was too late to help his brother though; Tom had been shot through the heart.

When he found that his brother was dead, Jack knelt beside him and cradled Tom's head in his arms, the tears running down his cheeks uncontrollably. His reaction though was as nothing to his mother's when she had slipped on a wrapper and come hurrying down to see what all the shooting was about. When Jenny saw her elder son's body and fully apprehended what had happened, she let out the most unearthly shriek and was then gripped by a paroxysm of grief. She slapped her own face like a mad woman and began rending her clothes, all the while making inarticulate sounds as though she were in agony. Jack's own sorrow was quite forgotten for the moment as he watched his mother behave like a crazy woman. She began to work herself into a positive frenzy, screaming and moaning as she grabbed hold of her dead son's hands and talked to him, telling him how much she loved him. All that Jack could do was kneel there, feeling bereft and utterly useless.

Until this moment, it had always been Jack who had turned to his mother for reassurance and support; it was strangely disconcerting now to find that the boot was on the other foot and that he was called upon, so he supposed, to comfort her. He put his arms awkwardly around her shoulders, but she didn't even notice, so preoccupied was she with the loss of her older son. Few mothers will admit it openly, but most have a favourite child, often their first, so it was with Jenny McAndrew. It was not that she loved Jack any less than Tom, but her first baby had a special place in her heart. When she had exhausted herself with all the crying and sobbing, she allowed Jack to help her to her feet and lead her back to the house. On the way, she stopped and found herself vomiting as a physical manifestation of her hysterical grieving. She was too wretched even to feel mortified by this action.

On the road back to Sawyer's Crossing, Abe Goldman said suddenly, 'Say, what happened to that gunpowder? You leave it behind?'

'Ah shit, so I did. No matter, we can always get some more if it's needful.'

'How's your arm?'

'I've had worse. It's only caught the muscle. It's a mercy that boy didn't come out of the house afore he fired or one of us could be dead by now.' Rutledge paused for a moment and then added, 'I've yet to thank you. That boy was getting the better of me. He was a tough one all right. I'm grateful to you for stopping him.'

'Oh, that don't signify,' said Goldman casually, as though gunning men down like that was the sort of thing he did every day of the week. 'I dare say as you'd've done the self-same thing for me if our positions had been reversed.'

Although he spoke lightly, killing that young man had been a hell of a thing for Abe Goldman. He'd always been one for getting the better of another man by words, rather than brute force. He'd been nervous as anything all the way up to McAndrew's Pass, fearful that he'd end up being shamed as a coward. That he had ended up rescuing a fellow like

45

Don Rutledge was a wonderful and wholly unlooked for turn of events. While he was musing about this, Rutledge said, 'There's no occasion to mention this to the boss.'

'What shall I say then?'

'Nothing. Tell him that we were fired on as we approached. Don't let on that it was only some kid as did this to me. I can't afford for to have anybody think I might be losing my edge.'

'Surely. I ain't about to blab.'

'That's the man. You keep quiet about this and I'll stand friend to you. We make a good combination. You ever kill a man before?'

Goldman didn't see any percentage in letting anybody know that this was the first time he'd even discharged a firearm in the direction of another human being, so he contented himself with remarking, 'When we get back, I'll lend you a hand digging out them pellets.'

It was hopeless trying to get his ma to go back to bed that night, so Jack just sat with her. He lit a lamp, stirred up the fire in the range and brewed some coffee. In a way, it was good that his mother was so distracted, because caring for her meant that he had no leisure to indulge himself in feeling his own sorrow at his beloved older brother's death.

That Tom had been his mother's favourite had been no particular secret and his brother and he had often joked about it. If permission was to be sought from their mother for some dubious scheme or other, it was always Tom who would approach her with the request. It was seldom that Jenny refused her elder son anything he desired. It might have been thought that this would create resentment in Jack, but there had never been anything of the kind. He too worshipped and idolized Tom and it seemed only natural to him that Ma would feel the same way.

Other than putting his arm round her shoulders where she sat at the kitchen table, there didn't appear to Jack that there was anything he could do to help his mother. She was shaking uncontrollably and breathing rapidly. He'd a notion that a shot of ardent spirits were what folk often relied upon under such circumstances, but there was none in the house and so he busied himself making sure that her cup was filled with sweet coffee. Hadn't he read somewhere that sugar was good when you'd had a shock?

There was no sleep for either Jack or his mother that night. The pale dawn light found them both still seated at the table. To his surprise, Jack had not cried again after those tears when first he knew that his brother was dead. The case was quite different for his ma; tears had been trickling down her cheeks in a more or less continuous stream all night long. Her face was ashen and her son was fearful for her health. He felt that this was one of those cases when women were needed, to sit and condole with the grieving woman, but he hesitated to leave her alone. He didn't put it into words, but at the back of his mind was the fear that she might harm herself if left alone; she was in that much of a state. So he just carried on sitting there at her side, from time to time muttering meaningless inanities along the lines of, 'It'll be all right, Ma,' and 'Don't take on so.'

CHAPTER 4

It was hard to tell whether Clarence Harper was pleased or dismayed at the news that his two deputies brought him the morning following the abortive raid on the farm at McAndrew's Pass. After Rutledge had given him an expurgated and edited version of the affair, Harper contented himself with remarking, 'So that older boy's dead, is that the strength of it?'

'That's right, sir,' said Abe Goldman obsequiously, 'Dead as the proverbial doornail.'

Harper thought this over for a minute and then said, 'I reckon that'll make our lives a little easier, at any rate. The younger boy couldn't have been above sixteen or seventeen years of age. He ain't likely to cause us any delay. Other than him, there's just the woman.'

'So what you want us to do, boss?' asked Rutledge, 'Go back there tonight?'

'Hell, no. We'll forge on ahead now and take it as

read that the family's out of the cart, as it were. Word'll get around the rest of the valley; the other farmers there will be lining up to sell us the little bits of land we need. Smart work, the both of you.'

After they'd left Harper, Don Rutledge said, 'I won't forget this, Goldman. You're a real friend.'

In fact, Abe Goldman was anything but Rutledge's friend. Ever since he picked up with the Rocky Mountains Railroad Company, he had been wondering how an oaf like Rutledge had managed to get himself into such an important position, acting in effect as Clarence Harper's right-hand man. The answer was, seemingly, that Rutledge appeared to get results. It didn't much matter to Harper how things were worked, just as long as difficulties were smoothed over and obstacles removed from his path. In the present situation, it wouldn't have mattered a tinker's damn whether one person or a dozen had been killed, or indeed, none at all. All that he cared about was that the line could continue onwards in the direction he had planned and that there would be no delays.

Thinking it over before he fell asleep that night, Goldman realized that he didn't have any bad conscience about killing the boy. He had been impelled to pull that trigger as much because he feared that once that rough character had finished with Rutledge, he might well turn his attentions to Rutledge's comrade. There had been a large

50

measure of self-interest involved. The other thing that had struck him was that it had been a clumsy, badly planned business. If they were going to kill somebody, why hazard their own bodies in that way? It would have made more sense to pay somebody to shoot one or both boys from a distance.

In short, Goldman was thinking of how he could supplant Don Rutledge as the man upon whom the boss depended. He'd an idea that if only Rutledge was out of the way and this railroad fetched up at that new port on schedule, then Harper might find him so indispensable that maybe he'd want to enter into something like a partnership.

About the same time that Goldman and Rutledge were leaving Harper's presence, Jack McAndrew was relieved to welcome a neighbour to his home. Habakkuk Jefferson farmed a stretch of land along the valley from the McAndrews and had heard the shots in the night. He had wanted to come at once to see what was happening, but his wife had forbidden him to set foot out of the house until morning. She was an exceedingly strong-willed woman and couldn't see the sense in her husband mixing himself up in something until he knew what was what.

When Jefferson had been apprised of the facts in the case, he shook his head sadly. 'I knowed there was trouble a brewin',' he said gloomily. 'I just knowed it. Eleven years we been settin' on that there land and I ain't yet found the spare money to go to law and register title to it. And so those bastards, beggin' your pardon, Mrs McAndrew, those devils have come by your house and done this? I don't know what the world's a' comin' to and that's a fact.'

As soon as the sun had risen, Jack McAndrew had left the house and retrieved his brother's body from where it was lying in the dirt. He wished that he could have brought it inside in a more dignified manner, but the fact was that it was all he could do to drag the corpse along into the barn. It felt mighty strange and disturbing to be hauling his brother around in that way, like he was a sack of potatoes or something.

Having got the corpse inside the barn, Jack thought it fitting not to leave it on the ground and so he managed to get it on the trestle table. His brother's eyes were open and staring and, despite his best efforts, Jack McAndrew found that he was unable to close the eyes. They were as stiff and unyielding as leather, the rigour having set in by this time. He found the sight of those blind eyes unnerving and so fished around in his pocket and, finding a couple of dimes, set those over the eyes to shield them from view. After Mr Jefferson had condoled with Jenny McAndrew, Jack led him to the barn to, as the farmer put it, 'Pay his respects' to Tom.

'Shot him in the back, hey?' said Jefferson, 'They must be a set of cowards. You say you saw 'em?'

'I did.'

52

'You certain-sure as they were connected with the railroad?'

'Yeah. I ran one of 'em off our land just a while earlier. I recognized him last night. Took a couple o' shots at him, but I don't know that I hit him.'

'You got sand, boy. What'll you do now?'

'Don't rightly know. Get justice for my brother, I guess.'

When he'd gone out to find Tom's body, there had been something curious near to it: a small, wooden keg. Judging from the length of fuse sticking out the top of this, it wasn't hard to figure that it was meant to be something in the nature of a mine and that the two men Tom had disturbed had most likely been planning to blow up their house while they slept. Jack had concealed the barrel of powder in the barn. If he had been in the slightest doubt about who had been behind the previous night's events, one look at the powder keg would have revealed the truth to him. Branded across the lid of the barrel were the words 'Property of the Rocky Mountains Railroad Company'. Jack hadn't seen any need to tell Habakkuk Jefferson about this. He'd an idea that it might come in handy at some point in the future.

Later that same day, Clarence Harper sent for Goldman and proceeded to question him closely about the likely legal aspects of the situation facing them over the McAndrews' property. His enquiries were practical and pragmatic, rather than touching upon the ethics of the affair. He said, 'What can that woman and her boy do legally to stop us laying our tracks 'cross their land?'

'In theory?' replied Abe Goldman. 'They have a watertight and unassailable case. They have absolute title to the land and we would be committing a tort if we so much as set our feet on that pasture we want, without their by-your-leave.'

This sounded unpromising enough, but Goldman's expression gave his boss to hope that the matter was not in reality as bleak for the company as the lawyer represented. Harper said, 'What steps would they need to take to enforce their rights?'

'It would cost them a hundred dollars or so, straight off. They'd have to apply to a judge in chambers for an emergency injunction to call a halt to our activity. The pleas would need to be set out by a lawyer, 'fore a judge would even consider it.'

'Hundred dollars, hey? Where would they find this judge? There ain't one in Sawyer's Crossing, I know that much.'

'They got a judge in Coulson, but that's nigh on fifty miles from here. Even once they get their injunction, they'd need to get a sheriff to enforce it for them. I don't see all this happening before we reach the pass.'

Clarence Harper mulled this over for a spell, a satisfied look upon his face. Then another thought occurred to him and he said, 'Say, what's to stop those folk simply standing guard with guns and preventing us from getting near?'

A wide grin split Abe Goldman's sharp face. 'Be downright illegal,' he told his boss happily. 'Conduct likely to cause a breach o' the peace. We'll swear out affidavits that will suggest that we have a legally binding agreement with the McAndrews and that we've paid them a monetary consideration for the use of their land.'

'You can draw up the papers for that?'

'Not the least problem. I'll do it this very day. Don't go near those two again though. I doubt that they'll have the wits to think about getting out an injunction against us. They're real rubes. Just leave 'em be now and then the first thing they'll know is when we fetch up with our crew.'

'You're worth your weight in gold, I tell you that much,' said Harper, and he meant it. As Abe Goldman was leaving, Harper called after him, 'Say, was it really you who shot that boy?'

'It really was.'

'I didn't think you had the balls for that kind of work. Happen I was wrong about you. Maybe you're good for the rough stuff as well as legal work.'

All of which was music to Abe Goldman's ears. This was just precisely the impression that he had been hoping to give to the boss and he left feeling greatly satisfied with himself. See if he didn't manage to replace that slow-witted clod Rutledge before long!

In his tent, Don Rutledge was brooding about the way in which things had gone wrong for him lately. He'd been ordered off that farm at gunpoint and humiliated in front of the boss and then that other boy had beaten up on him. To cap it all, he'd needed to be rescued by that pale little clerk. Although he had no idea that Goldman was after his position in the company, Rutledge knew that he'd need to do something pretty damned soon to show that he wasn't losing his grip. Once a man started to slip down in the estimation of others, it was necessary to take sharp corrective action to demonstrate how mistaken they were in thinking that you were no longer a force to be reckoned with.

It was quite true that Jack McAndrew was only a simple country boy with no more familiarity with the law of property than he had of the conditions on the planet Mars, but that didn't mean that he was a perfect fool. It was just common sense that if you had something that others wanted, then they would try and take it from you. If they couldn't do this by force, then they might resort to other means. Money had been offered and declined and this had been followed by violence. What this suggested to Jack was that the next step would entail some species of legal trickery. He knew nothing of the law, but a good deal about ordinary human nature.

Although he was grief-stricken at the loss of his big

brother, there was little point in moping around and bemoaning his fate. It was now up to him, Jack McAndrew, to save the farm from those grasping villains. A first step, as far as he was able to see, might be trying to bring the murder of his brother home to those who had committed it by having them arrested. He could offer a good description of one of the men who was involved in the crime and he had some solid evidence that showed the railroad company to be involved. But first, he needed to tend to his mother and see that she was being safely looked after.

Before he left, Mr Jefferson himself had tentatively advanced the idea that Jenny McAndrew might wish to stay with him and his family for a day or two. This sounded a good scheme to Jack. He would, he supposed, have to arrange for Tom's burial in the next few days and did not know whether he first needed to report the death to somebody official. He would be seeing a sheriff that day, God willing, and so that might be a good time to discuss what was needful in order to fix up the funeral.

His mother was so bowed down with her loss that she made no objection to being bundled up into the buckboard and driven over to the Jeffersons' place. Mrs Jefferson might be a hard-featured and uncompromising woman who generally had things her own way, but she had a kind heart behind her forbidding exterior – at least as far as other women were concerned.

'Lord a' mercy,' cried Mrs Jefferson, who was working in her kitchen garden when the buckboard arrived. 'My Hab, he told me the whole tale. I never heared the like, I tell you straight.' She left her hoe and went over to where Jack's mother was standing by the cart, looking utterly lost and bereft. 'Just you come into the house now, Jennifer, and we'll see what's to do. You stay here just as long as you please, you hear what I tell you now?'

Mr Jefferson came out to speak a few words to Jack. He said, 'What you a' goin' to do now, boy?'

Jack shrugged, as though he had no clear plans. 'I reckon as I'll tidy up back at our place and make for to get the funeral fixed up. Happen I should ride over to Sawyer's Crossing today or tomorrow and inform the sheriff what passed.'

Habakkuk Jefferson snorted derisively. 'If'n you're lucky enough to catch Mort Williams when he ain't at the faro table, then I guess that scheme might not altogether miscarry.'

'I'll see what's to do.'

The truth was that Jack McAndrew knew exactly what he was going to be doing. The death of his brother and the state to which this had reduced his beloved mother had awoken a terrible longing in the youngster's breast to be revenged upon the men he'd seen the night before, them and their boss, too. All three were answerable for this tragedy and he was the one to make sure that they paid in full.

That evening, while Jack was sorting out one or two things and preparing for his trip into Sawyer's Crossing, the business manager of the Rocky Mountains Railroad Company was looking to salvage his self-respect and make up for the gross humilation of being rescued from a fight by a lawyer. Don Rutledge was in a dangerous mood and those with any sense were giving him a very wide berth.

The Tanglefoot was crowded and Rutledge wasn't too sure where he should start. To be more precise, he wasn't sure *who* he should start on. Rutledge had always found that a sovereign remedy for feeling low was to pick a fight with some hapless individual and then beat him to a pulp. After the fiasco up at McAndrew's Pass though, he didn't rightly know if that would do tonight. He had it in mind to shed blood publicly, which would definitely show all those in the saloon, as well as those who later heard about it, that they would do well to steer clear of Don Rutledge.

Although Rutledge was feeling well disposed towards Abe Goldman, he didn't want him around for this little exhibition. He'd seen no evidence to suggest that it was so, but Rutledge was anxious lest the lawyer had begun to put on side about rescuing him from that bastard up at the pass. He wanted to brace and then deal with some victim without

Goldman being around and perhaps thinking that he should get into the habit of pulling Rutledge's chestnuts out of the fire.

In the end, Don Rutledge selected a mean-looking customer who was standing at the bar. He wasn't one of the men working on the railroad and could presumably be beaten black and blue without any long term consequences. From what Abe Goldman had said to him, the sheriff in this town was, in any case, beholden in some way to the boss and was likely to overlook a spot of violence. Picking a fight in the saloon wasn't at all hard. Rutledge provoked it by the time-honored expedient of going up alongside his target and carefully positioning a clay pipe on the bar at his elbow. Then it was simply a matter of waiting for the fellow to make the wrong movement and send it flying to smash on the floor.

It only took a minute for the man Rutledge had chosen to assuage his feelings, to wave his arms about unguardedly and knock the pipe off the bar. He didn't even notice that he had done so until Don Rutledge tapped him on the shoulder and said, 'You broke my favourite pipe.'

'I broke your pipe? What in the hell are you talkin' about?'

Rutledge pointed without speaking to the shattered fragments of the pipe, where they lay at the man's feet.

'That was your favourite pipe?' asked the man in

disbelief, a smile beginning to spread across his face. 'It's no more than an old clay pipe as you've had since last week at most. I know all those dodges for starting trouble. You want a fight, you come to the right shop. You don't have to make up stories about pipes.'

'You calling me a liar?' asked Rutledge.

The man he was goading didn't even bother to reply, but instead, tossed the contents of his glass into Rutledge's face and then took a swing at him. He was a little too slow, because even as he drew back his arm, Rutledge ducked and the man's blow went wide, knocking the drink from another man's hand. This individual, not being the sort of fellow to allow such liberties, turned round at once and punched the man Rutledge had picked on, hard in the stomach, causing him to fold up like a pocket rule.

For the next five minutes things were pretty lively in the Tanglefoot saloon, as stranger traded blow with stranger, until those fighting ran out of energy. The barkeep shouted at them to calm down and quit breaking up the place, but this made little difference and the brawl died down eventually of its own accord. Rutledge felt exhilarated by the brief burst of physical violence and succeeded in landing a number of vicious kicks and punches upon men quite unknown to him. He began to feel like his old self again and was in fair way towards forgetting about the embarrassment of the last couple of days.

Had he left it there, matters might have ended reasonably, with no more harm done than a few bloody noses and the odd black eye, but it was simply not in Don Rutledge's nature to end on a sensible note. As the fighting petered out, he observed that the man he had originally tried to pick a quarrel with had no present adversary and was just standing there, looking pleased with himself. Rutledge picked up a heavy chair and swung it over his head, felling the other man like pole-axed ox.

The consequences of Rutledge's assault on the stranger in the saloon were far-reaching and unexpected, not least for the victim himself. Don Rutledge had been knocked about in enough roughhouses not to regard being sent sprawling to the sawdust-covered floor of a saloon as anything special. It was the sort of thing which happened to men when they went drinking. What he didn't realize was that he had, quite by chance, swung that chair right at the crucial angle to effect serious mischief to the fellow whose head he had struck. It was sheer bad luck. A fraction of an inch further to one side or the other and it would most likely have ended up with a man waking up the next day with a pounding headache all but indistinguishable from a severe hangover. In the event, the man wasn't in a position to wake up at all the next day, because his neck had been broken as neatly and cleanly as though he had been hanged.

The knocking of a man senseless with a chair was

not altogether unknown in the Tanglefoot and at first, nobody thought much of it. When the man showed no signs of stirring though, somebody thought to kneel down and check that he was all right. This man put his ear to the prone figure's mouth and then felt for a pulse in his neck. After checking carefully, he looked up at Rutledge and said in surprise, 'Hey, you know what? You done killed him!'

CHAPTER 5

There were, as Jack McAndrew saw it, two things that clearly linked the Rocky Mountains Railroad Company with his brother's death. The first of these was very simply that he had seen one of the men who was present at the death of his brother, here at the farm, in the company of that damned rascal Clarence Harper. Suppose that this was not regarded by the sheriff of Sawyer's Crossing as solid and reliable evidence? Well then, there was that keg of powder which the men who killed his brother had left behind when they fled.

Jack hefted the barrel in his hand and it was then that it occurred to him that, if things got nasty, he would perhaps be able to find a use for this gunpowder in the future. He would be a fool to hand it over to Mort Williams. After all, it was the keg itself which bore the railroad company's name, not the powder which it contained. A quick search of the kitchen unearthed a large earthenware pitcher which would hold the powder if Jack tipped it out. He did so and then covered the pitcher carefully and put it where a stray spark would not be likely to land in it and blow him to kingdom come.

It was Jack's intention while reporting the death of his brother and letting the sheriff know that the funeral would be taking place, to see if he couldn't lay responsibility for Tom's death squarely where it belonged: with the Rocky Mountains Railroad Company. His brother had been murdered and his mother broken down with the grief of it. Surely, it would be possible to see those who had carried out the murder brought to justice?

For a short time after the death, Jack had been consumed with thoughts of vengeance and envisaged riding after the men who had laid Tom low and exacting bloody revenge single-handedly by himself. But when once he had calmed down a little, he saw that as an act of madness. How would his mother react if he got himself killed in the process? Besides which, he wasn't at all sure that he was capable of going up against ruthless killers of the kind who had shot Tom. No, the sensible dodge would be to report the case to the sheriff and see that he handled the matter according to the law.

Having decided this, there was no point in failing to make preparations of his own and ensure that he was properly protected against any violence which might be tried on his own person. Those men were dead set on gaining a piece of land from this farm and they had shown that they would stop at nothing in their endeavours to do so. After he had collected his brother's body from where it had been lying outside the house, Jack had gone back and picked up the Colt Navy that Tom had carried. He had laid this on the trestle table, next to his brother's corpse. Now, Jack had second thoughts about the wisdom of interring a perfectly good pistol with his brother. He might have need of that weapon before he was finished.

As he carried the lamp across the yard to the barn, it struck him that there might perhaps be something a mite creepy about seeing a dead body at night. It had been one thing the night before, when there had been so much going on, but now he was alone on the farm, just him and a corpse. Surprisingly though, he didn't feel spooked. The barn was cavernous and dark; the feeble glow from the lamp scarcely reached the corners. And there, right in the middle, stood the table upon which his brother lay. Jack walked up slowly to the improvised bier and stared. Fond as he had been of his brother, he found, to his surprise, that he felt nothing. Whatever else was here in the barn, his brother was not present. Jack didn't even know if he truly believed in the life after death of which the preachers told, but he was pretty sure that this cold chunk of flesh had little to do with the living, breathing, warm person who had inhabited it until a matter of hours before. It was no more than an empty husk.

Without stopping, the young man reached out and picked up the pistol that his brother had carried since the death of their father. He figured that if any living person now had a right to wear this iron, then it had to be him.

One of the first moves that Abe Goldman had made when he had been taken on by the Rocky Mountains Railroad Company was to persuade his new boss to part with $500. Clarence Harper had been none too happy about handing over this money, not seeing the need to do so.

'What the hell are you talking about?' Harper had asked in amazement, when the lawyer had put forward the idea, 'Why should I make a gift of five hundred dollars to the sheriff of Sawyer's Crossing, just answer me that?'

'Because he'll be beholden to us,' explained Goldman patiently. 'If there's any trouble when our boys hit town, he'll not be in a position to be too hard on them. Or us.'

'I still don't get it,' Harper had said stubbornly. 'I can see the sense in bribing a man when there's need. I do that anyway, to grease the wheels and keep 'em turning. But giving money up front like this? It doesn't make any sort of sense. I ain't a millionaire, you know. Leastways, not yet.'

In the end, Harper had handed over the cash and Goldman had ridden ahead of the crew to Sawyer's Crossing, which they were due to reach in another two weeks, and sought out Sheriff Mort Williams. Before doing so, he had spent an afternoon in the local saloon, just listening to gossip. When, later that day, he had popped into the sheriff's office, Goldman had had a pretty good idea of what sort of man he was dealing with. Popular opinion had Mort Williams pegged for a gambler, a man addicted to the faro table. That was good, men with weaknesses are always easier to deal with. So it was that Abe Goldman had pressed the $500 on Williams, begging him to use it for any charitable concern in which he had an interest. The lawyer represented this as a slight compensation in advance for any sort of inconvenience which the arrival in his town of a crew of navigators might cause to Sheriff Williams.

Without stating the case in so many words, Abe Goldman had managed to convey to the sheriff that the money which he had handed him was really in the nature of a bribe and that he had no expectation that it would really find its way anywhere other than to Mort Williams's own pocket. The sheriff had signed for receipt of the money and the matter was concluded.

Two weeks later and the railroad had reached town and Abe Goldman was congratulating himself on his prescience. Now there are things which a bribe can help with and cause a lawman to look the other way: somebody in gaol for fighting in public, or even an alleged assault on a woman, can often be smoothed over by the passing of a wad of bills under the table. Some trouble though, cannot be so easily disposed of. There are very few sheriffs prepared to turn a blind eye to murder, to give one obvious example. It was now that the lawyer's foresight was to prove invaluable.

Unfortunately for Rutledge, his final attack on the hapless fellow whom he had targeted in the Tanglewood, had taken place just when everybody else had stopped fighting. There was accordingly no shortage of witnesses to his savage assault with the piece of furniture which resulted in the death of the man. It was as clear-cut a case of homicide as one could hope to see and the sheriff was left with little choice but to arrest Rutledge as soon as the crime was reported to him. Mort Williams was uneasily aware that he had benefited from the largesse of the Rocky Mountains Railroad Company, but there really was little that he could do in this particular case.

The morning after the death in the saloon found Mort Williams behind his desk at front of the sheriff's office and Don Rutledge locked up in the cell in the room at the back. The door to the street opened and in walked the man who had handed over all that money a few weeks earlier. Abe Goldman looked jolly and cheerful, as if he didn't have a care in the world. There was good reason for this: he knew that his hand was unbeatable and that whatever this small-town, hick lawman laid down, Goldman would be able to beat it.

When he'd heard that Rutledge had been arrested for murder, Goldman had considered letting him rot in gaol and making his own play for promotion to Rutledge's job right then and there. He decided against it though. The boss relied heavily upon his business manager and Goldman would gain more credit from having him freed than he would from pretending that there was nothing to be done. There was no hurry, anyway. He knew that he would be supplanting Rutledge some time soon whatever the outcome of this little episode might be.

As soon as he recognized Goldman, Sheriff Williams began his protestations before the other man had even had a chance to speak. 'I'm sorry, there's nothing I can do about this. That man I took into custody was seen by a dozen witnesses to kill a man at the Tanglefoot last night. It's nigh-on an open-and-shut case. I can't just brush it under the carpet.'

'Sheriff,' said Goldman, in apparent bewilderment, 'I have not the remotest idea what you're talking about! What's all this about a man in custody?'

'One o' your boys. Got mixed up in a fight. Started

it, from all that I am able to collect.'

Abe Goldman shook his head disapprovingly. 'Lordy, the things folk get up to. What I need from you is nothing to do with any fight. You recollect that money I gave you a while back?'

Mort Williams nodded. 'Yes, of course I do. You told me to give it to some charitable undertaking.'

'That's precisely right,' said Goldman, smiling, 'Thing is, I now find that for tax purposes, I need to know just exactly where you put the money. I'm telling you, the tax people are the most suspicious bunch of men you ever did hear tell of. 'Less I dot all my I's and cross all my T's, they'll be suspecting all sorts of trickery. If you could just give me the address of the people you handed that donation over to?'

This was a tricky question, because, as Mort Williams very well knew and Abe Goldman strongly suspected, the sheriff had lost every last cent of that money at the faro table within forty-eight hours of receiving it. The sheriff sat there for a matter of seconds, his mouth opening and closing like a landed catfish gasping for air. At length, Goldman said pleasantly, 'Hey, that's all right. Don't worry if you haven't yet donated the money anywhere. Just let me have it back and we'll work out where to send it.'

There was dead silence in the office as it gradually dawned on Sheriff Mort Williams just what was going on here. He said, 'I don't have the money any more.'

Goldman's voice took on a sharper edge as he

asked, 'Don't have it? Where'd it go?'

'Spent it,' mumbled the sheriff.

'Spent it, did you? Our company gave you that money in good faith as a gesture of our intentions. It wasn't a personal gift, you know. What did you think, that we were offering you a bribe or something?'

This was, of course, both what Mort Williams had thought and also what had in fact happened when the $500 was handed over. He said nothing. After another period of silence, Abe Goldman said briskly, 'I have your signature on a receipt for that money. It strikes me, Sheriff, that what we're looking at here is a clear case of malfeasance in public office. Looks to me as though you have been diverting public money into your own pocket. I needn't tell you, I suppose, that public officials go to gaol for that?'

'I'll pay it back. I'll pay it all back.' Mort Williams was hoping to retire in another year or two. The prospect of ending up in gaol was the worst thing that he could imagine. He was prepared to do anything at all to avoid it.

'All right, let's stop fooling around,' said Abe Goldman, 'Here's how things stand: You don't set free my friend right this second, I'm going to swear out an affidavit against you this very day, charging you with corruption.'

Sheriff Williams was defeated. Without a word, he stood up and removed a key from his pocket. Then he went into the back room, from where he emerged

72

a minute later accompanied by Don Rutledge. Before Rutledge and Goldman left the office, the lawyer said, 'Just so we understand each other, I have your signature on a receipt for five hundred dollars. It's plain evidence of corruption. Until we have moved on from this town, you help us all you can. Then, when we leave, you can forget about us. Deal?'

'Deal,' said Williams, utterly defeated.

Clarence Harper was more effusive than Goldman had ever seen him before. Harper was not in the habit of praising his subordinates, figuring that keeping them worried about their jobs was a better way of ensuring that they worked hard, but today he was expansive. 'Goldman, you are a wonder-worker!' he declared, when the lawyer walked into Harper's tent with Rutledge in tow. 'How in the hell did you manage to get the sheriff to release this rascal?'

The little lawyer was never averse to demonstrating his own cleverness to others and in this case, he was also able to show how he had been right and his boss wrong about handing over the bribe a fortnight earlier. 'See now,' he explained, 'if I hadn't given that fellow the money before and let him have a chance to gamble it away, we'd never have got Don here out of gaol. Sheriff Williams could have told me to get lost if I'd tried to offer him a bribe after he'd made the arrest. Hell, he could even have arrested me for trying to influence him. As it is, well, he's ours until we move on.'

'I'll say it again,' said Harper, 'you are a regular genius!' He turned to Rutledge, 'Ain't that so? I reckon you're feeling mighty obliged to Goldman here?'

'I surely am. Thanks, Abe. I truly appreciate your help.'

'Ah, you would've done just the same for me if the tables had been turned,' said the lawyer. 'We all got our different talents.' What he didn't say, but hoped that Clarence Harper would recollect, was that Goldman was not only useful at springing people from gaol, as he had done this day, but that he was a man of action too, having rescued Rutledge from another tricky situation by means of gunplay. There was no doubt in Goldman's mind that his star was in the ascendant.

After Goldman and Rutledge had left his office, Mort Williams was feeling so upset and disturbed, that he broke his ironclad rule and treated himself to a shot of whiskey from the bottle he kept for 'medicinal purposes', right that minute, rather than doing as he usually did and waiting until finishing work before imbibing liquor. He had no sooner gulped down a generous measure of the soothing liquid, when the door to the street opened again and a young man, scarcely more than a boy, entered his office.

'How can I help you, son?' asked the sheriff, feeling more at ease now that he was dealing with a greenhorn kid, rather than those tricky devils from the railroad company.

'Well, sir,' began Jack hesitantly, 'I'd like to report a death. Well, a murder really.'

As soon as the boy opened his mouth, Williams had a terrible feeling of foreboding and somehow knew that this also was mixed up in some fashion with the doings of the Rocky Mountains Railroad Company. His worst suspicions were swiftly confirmed when the youngster told of the death of his brother, giving a word picture of his murderer which tallied in every last detail with the appearance and character of the man who had lately been lodged in the cell at the back of the sheriff's office. Then, to round matters off, a wooden powder keg was produced, with the name of the railroad company stamped on the top of the barrel.

There was only one thing for it, at least as far as Mort Williams was concerned, and that was to lie like the Devil. 'I'm mighty grateful to you for reporting this death,' he told Jack. 'Not everybody bothers with such formalities. You may be sure that I'll make a record of this and look into the circumstances.'

'What are you going to do?' asked the young man.

'Do? Like I told you, I'm going to look into it. Don't try and crowd me now, because it won't answer. I'm the sheriff of this town. It's for me to decide what's needful.'

'What about this keg? Why, it's even got the name

75

of the company on it, the outfit which that man worked for.'

'Yes, I'll allow as that's material evidence, which is why I'm a going to take charge of it. Hand it over. I'll make investigations. Now, if there's nothing else, I got a heap of work to do.'

Young and inexperienced as he was, it was tolerably plain to Jack McAndrew that the sheriff of Sawyer's Crossing was receiving news of a murder in a very casual way. So casually, that it didn't look to the young man sitting opposite him as though he was proposing to take any action at all. McAndrew said, 'Thank you for your time, Sheriff. I can bury my brother then?'

Williams waved his arm dismissively and said, 'Yes, yes. You go right ahead son. Sorry for your loss and all.'

When once he was outside the sheriff's office and back on the boardwalk, Jack stopped and considered what his next step should be. One thing was for sure: if he wanted justice for his brother then there was no point in waiting for that old fellow to help him; he would be obliged to settle the matter by his own self.

While the young man was standing there, uncertain what to do next, Clarence Harper was setting out to his assistants just how he saw things progressing in the next week or so. 'We're going to press ahead past that little town, soon as may be. Then we should reach McAndrew's Pass in ten days if those damned coolies put their backs into it. We'll drive right past the farmhouse and then along by the cliff until we reach the open country leading to Fort Benton. None of the other spreads in that valley has been proved up on. We got as much right to lay tracks over it as those small-time farmers have to plant crops.'

'There's the mother and one more boy living in the house,' Goldman reminded his boss. 'You want that we should move them out first?'

'No point. How old's the boy?'

'Sixteen, maybe seventeen at most,' said Rutledge.

'There you are. He'll run when he sees our boys coming towards 'em.'

'I ain't so sure,' said Rutledge thoughtfully, 'it was him who ran us off the farm before.'

'Yes,' said Harper tartly, 'I remember well enough. I'm not liable to forget in a hurry either. It's not every day that some snot-nosed kid with a squirrel gun gives me orders. It'll be fine. You'll see.'

After they'd been dismissed from the boss's presence, Goldman and Rutledge wandered back to their own tent. The air was filled with the hammering of the gangs as they laid down the rails. Another day or two and they would actually be in Sawyer's Crossing at this rate.

'You think the boss is right about that boy?' asked Rutledge.

'Don't see what we can do if he isn't,' replied Abe

Goldman diplomatically, unwilling to be heard criticizing Clarence Harper, even by implication, 'I'm game if you want to take some little action about him on the quiet.'

Rutledge gave his companion a quick glance and said, 'No, I reckon it's as Mr Harper says. We'll just fetch up at this farm and do what we need.' He didn't say out loud that he was feeling aggrieved that, once again, Goldman had had to get him out of a fix and he didn't much want to undertake any further adventures with the other man. It always seemed to end with Goldman's reputation being enhanced as his own was tarnished in the sight of their boss.

CHAPTER 6

The weeks following his brother's murder and funeral were busy ones for Jack McAndrew. He knew, after his interview with Sheriff Williams, that he could expect nothing to be done by that individual by way of investigation into Tom's death. Jack didn't precisely understand the whys and wherefores of the case, but there it was. In a dime novel, he would have strapped on his dead brother's gun and gone out to seek vengeance single-handed, but that was all a lot of nonsense and fortunately Jack McAndrew had the wit to know it. All that remained was to ensure that Tom's death had not been in vain and that the railroad company did not drive through their land.

One of the most dangerous things about young men of seventeen or eighteen is that they have little sense of proportion. When they set out on a course of action, they will go just that little bit too far and take far wilder actions than a fellow of more mature years might be inclined to do. Which is why some of the deadliest killers and gunfighters began slaying men over fancied slights when they were still barely men. John Wesley Hardin and Billy the Kid spring to mind. Jack McAndrews was not a natural born killer and if the Rocky Mountains Railroad Company hadn't pushed him in that way, he would most likely have lived in McAndrew's Pass his whole life long, tending the crops and looking after his mother in old age. As it was, before the dawn of his eighteenth birthday, he was fated to carry out the worst massacre ever seen in the United States outside of wartime: a direct consequence of that lack of proportion which afflicts so many youngsters. Jack had a grudge against one or two men, but his actions brought about the deaths of dozens.

Jack and his mother could see the railroad inching towards their land a week before it actually arrived. After they had buried Tom near the house, Jenny McAndrew had come home. Don Rutledge was driving the coolies hard and they were managing to lay down the tracks at a rate in excess of a mile a day. Following Harper's directions, Rutledge and Goldman were simply ignoring the farmers who lined the valley of McAndrew's Pass. The rails would be laid down across the land which lay beside the cliffs of the Sweetwater Mountains and if anybody opposed them, well, they would be dealt with.

It was a gloomy, overcast day, when Jack said to his

mother, 'Ma, I have to go off for the morning. Up into the mountains.'

'We got a heap o' work to be done, son. There's no time for moping around and thinking of what's done and past.'

Since the funeral of her elder son, Jenny McAndrew was like a mechanical toy in which the spring had been broken. She was listless and apathetic; allowed her young son to make decisions about the farm and also any plans for the future. From time to time, she would be roused to something like her old self, which was what was happening this day, when Jack talked of going up into the Sweetwaters.

'I ain't a' goin' to be moping round, Ma,' he told her, 'nor thinking about what's done and past neither.' He smiled at her. 'I'm thinking' 'bout the future, like what happens when those blamed railroad men come to lay their tracks outside our windows.'

'Not much to be done about it. If your father had been spared. . . . Or maybe if Tom was here. . . .'

'Well, they ain't. It's just me and I'm going to see what I can do.'

Along the floor of the mountain pass, the land was level and smooth. It was especially so right at the foot of the towering cliffs on the north side of the valley, which was where the railroad men were seemingly minded to run the line. The other side was hopeless, being boggy and covered in rocks and boulders. No, they would certainly hope to use the flat land and take their damned railroad right along there, about a dozen feet from the back wall of the farmhouse. Well, not if Jack McAndrew had anything to do with it they wouldn't!

In most places along the north side of the valley, the cliffs were almost sheer, soaring to a hundred feet or so above the farmland below. In one place though, just after you entered the pass, the rock face leaned forward, forming a slight overhang. Jack recalled his father telling his sons that one day the rain and frost would loosen that rock and the whole cliff face would come tumbling down onto their fields. Jack, who had been only eight or nine at the time, had looked up fearfully and clutched his father's hand. 'Will it happen soon?' he had asked.

His father had laughed and told him that in the natural way of things, he didn't look for that cliff to come tumbling down for at least a thousand years or more. They could all rest easy in their own lifetimes.

That cliff might not fall for centuries, if left to its own devices, but what if it was given a little help and assistance in that direction? It must be said that young Jack McAndrew's aim was not to kill a bunch of men, but merely to divert the railroad; perhaps create such inconvenience that the company would think twice about coming through there. It was a madcap and ill-considered scheme, but it must be borne in mind that he was no more than a callow boy. To him, it made perfect sense.

It took some time to climb along the cliffs and reach a point right on top of the overhang in which he was interested and, as soon as he did so, McAndrew noticed something very curious. The rock behind the section of overhanging cliff was lined with crevices and deep channels. These had perhaps originally been cut by running water, but over the millennia, frost and ice had got into the cracks and widened them, until some were perhaps twenty feet deep and three or four feet wide. One in particular caught Jack's eye. It ran for fully fifty feet parallel to the edge of the cliff. If that miniature chasm could be enlarged and split, then surely half the overhanging cliff face would break away and fall right into the path of the projected railroad line. The crevice was deep enough for Jack to climb into and explore and the more he examined it, the better suited it appeared to be for his purpose.

After having established that this was just what he had been hoping to discover, the young man clambered out of the crevice and stood on the very edge of the cliff looking east. In the distance, he could just make out the tents of the navigators who were building the railroad by the sweat of their brows. They had forged on past Sawyer's Crossing now and were perhaps five or six miles from where he was standing. At this rate, he thought moodily, they would be here inside a week.

When he got back home, Jack found his mother sitting at the kitchen table, staring into space. It broke his heart to see her so; a woman who was, in the usual way of things, always so active and busy. 'Ma,' he said, sitting down opposite her, 'I think it would do you good to go and stay with your folks in Fort Benton.'

Jenny McAndrew looked up at her son. 'Lordy, Jack, I couldn't do such a thing. There's a heap o' things need doing here.'

'I can manage the place by myself, Ma,' the boy told her. 'Truly I can. We're goin' to need to get a hired man in anyway. I can arrange that while you're gone.'

It was clear from the look on her face that the grieving woman found the idea of being away from the farm for a while attractive, but still she hesitated. Jack said gently, 'You need to be away from here for a space. Memories.... Please go and stay with your sister. You know you want to really.'

The ghost of smile flickered across her lips, the first time she had smiled since Tom had died. 'Don't coax, Jack,' Jenny said, with something of her usual asperity, 'I'll make up my own mind. Still and all, there is somewhat to say for the idea. You really could manage here without me for a spell?'

'I ain't a kid any more, you know.'

'No,' his mother said sadly, 'that you're not. All

right, maybe I will venture up to Fort Benton for a week or two. You won't get up to any mischief in my absence, I hope and trust?'

'Ma, I'm seventeen!'

So it was that three days after this conversation, Habakkuk Jefferson arrived with his wagon and took Jack's mother off to Fort Benton, leaving the boy in control of the house and farm. During the course of those three days, Jack had suffered agonies of impatience as the railroad crept ever closer to their home. He surely couldn't take any wild action with his mother setting at home not a mile from where he proposed to carry out his mad actions.

As soon as Jenny was clear of the place, the first thing that Jack did was fetch out the earthenware pitcher containing the ten pounds of fine powder which he had removed from the keg left behind by the railroad men. He was no military engineer, but if he couldn't fashion some sort of mine or petard from this quantity of explosives, then his name wasn't Jack McAndrew.

The method of progression used by the men building the railroad was simple and practical. Nobody could ever have guessed that such a well-organized system would end up killing three-dozen men. Each morning, while most of the men started work on laying tracks, another group would pack up the tents and so on and then ride on ahead to pitch them about a mile forward of the point where the work was beginning that day. Then, when the day's work was finally over, they could just collapse in their tents, without having to erect them when they were dog-tired. The chuck-wagon also moved up, so that the evening meal was ready and waiting for them at the end of the day.

Don Rutledge and Abe Goldman were above such lowly activities as shifting tents and chivvying along those in charge of the chuck-wagon. They sat side by side on their horses that morning, watching the activity. The camp was like a disturbed ants' nest each morning, with hundred of coolies rushing hither and thither about their various jobs.

'Well,' said Goldman, 'I reckon day after tomorrow, we'll be fetching up in the pass. You think it'll go smoothly?'

'Hard to say. I'd reckon so though. Less'n that boy can rally the squatters further up the valley and get them to combine with him in fightin'. Even then, we got enough firepower to deal with 'em. Can't see none o' them goin' to law about it either.'

'Happen you're right. There's something about that boy though. . . .' He let his voice tail off.

'I know what you mean,' said Rutledge. 'I felt it when he ran me and the boss off their land. He was only a kid with a squirrel gun, but I thought he would'a shot us had we resisted.'

'Well, we'll see in another day or two.'

86

'I'm minded to ride up that way tomorrow, just to set the boy on the right path and see that he means no mischief to us. Couldn't do any harm.'

'You want I should come with you?' asked Goldman. 'Two can do better than one, sometimes.'

'No, you're right. I don't look for trouble from him.'

Jack McAndrew's plan was harebrained enough, but it contained a seed of good sense. He knew enough about railroads to know that the lines   couldn't make any sharp turns and that they changed direction slowly and gracefully, tracing wide arcs. If he were to bring down that cliff when the workers were still miles off, they might be able to adjust the course and so curve gently around the obstacle that he hoped to create. If, however, he brought about the blockage when the line was almost entering the pass, then any deviation that was taken would be certain-sure to bring the line across the swampy and boggy ground to the south. The space between the cliffs was very narrow at that point; no more than half a mile separated the rock faces as you entered the pass.

One thing that the youngster knew was that gunpowder has to be closely contained and pressed close if it is going to explode with any force. A heap of powder out in the open that has a light applied to it will not explode, but rather flare up in a brief burst of fire. It is only when it is in a solid container that

87

gunpowder can be persuaded actually to explode, rather than merely burn. The stouter the vessel in which the powder is enclosed, the greater the force of the resulting explosion. When they were a little younger, Jack and his brother had, like so many youngsters, experimented with home-made bombs and discovered these basic rules for theirselves.

So it was that at dawn of the day following Don Rutledge expressing his intention to come up and see what was happening on the McAndrews's place, Jack set off up a path leading into the mountains with a metal can into which he had poured the powder. Protruding from the spout was the long fuse that he had found at the same time as the keg of gunpowder.

It took Jack an hour to reach the spot at which he was aiming, the long, deep crevice that he had explored a few days previously. He was so puffed out when he reached the spot, that he didn't feel that he had the energy for climbing further and peering over the edge of the cliff to where the railroad men were working, a mile and a half off from his home. He had gauged the distance well enough from his house that morning before setting off. All the workers were a mile or more from his activitites; or so he thought.

Had he taken the time and trouble to scramble up the slope from the crevice into which he was descending, he would have seen something curious. A team of forty coolies was busy erecting a village of tents at the foot of the cliff. The Chinese worked quietly and industriously, with none of the shouting and cursing which one would have heard from a bunch of white men engaged in a similar task. While the Chinese men worked, a white man sat on his horse watching them, a moody and discontented look on his face.

From time to time, Rutledge yelled at the men working so quickly and efficiently to erect the tents. 'Liven your ideas up, you slant-eyed bastards!' he shouted. His heart was not in this more or less automatic abuse though, because he was preoccupied with two problems. The first of these concerned Abe Goldman.

There was no doubt that Harper's business manager was possessed of many qualities which made him an invaluable tool for his boss. Intellectual ability was not however chief among the features of Rutledge's character which recommended him as a useful employee of the Rocky Mountains Railroad Company. In short, he was a dab hand with a gun, would stick at nothing and had no conscience to speak of. But he was not bright.

Dull-witted as he was though, it was gradually dawning on him that the lawyer who had been so friendly and agreeable to him was perhaps after his job. It had taken him longer than it would some men to realize this, but now that he was sure in his own mind that this was what was going on, he knew that the neatest and most economical solution to the problem would be to kill Goldman as soon as possible; perhaps even that very day.

The other thing taxing Rutledge's brain was what to do about that young fellow up at the farm; which lay just a half mile from where he was currently placed. Rutledge was not a superstitious man, but at the same time, he believed in certain powers beyond the reach of our knowledge. There was, for example, what he thought of as the 'rule of three'. Things oftentimes tended to come along in threes, as he had noticed time and again in his life. This applied to hearing an unusual word, coming across an acquaintance and many other things in life. In the present instance, he had been run off by that young man at the point of a gun, then he had actually been shot at by the boy and now he was due to go and see him once more – for the third time. At the back of Rutledge's mind, absurd though it was, was the fear that his third encounter with the kid might end in his own death.

It was for this reason that right now, Rutledge felt more inclined to sit on his horse cursing the coolies than he was to go riding up to the farmhouse that he could see in the distance. He honestly had a bad feeling about it; the feeling that his next encounter with that wretched youth might prove fatal to himself.

Had he been aware of what Jack was up to that very

second, it is to be doubted whether Don Rutledge would have been in any way reassured. The young man was at the bottom of the crevice which he had chosen and was placing the can containing the ten pounds of powder in a crack on the floor of the little chasm in which he was squatting. Having wedged the can in there, McAndrew went off to collect as many rocks as he could find. These, he piled up on top of the can. The more closely was the explosion confined, the more powerful it was apt to be.

It was quiet in the crevice, something like the hush that one encounters in an empty church. Certainly, Jack McAndrew could not hear any noise from the toiling coolies, nor even Rutledge's occasional angry shouting at them.

When he had brought all the rocks that he could find and buried the can of powder beneath them, the boy unrolled the fuse which he had placed in the can and stretched it out as far as it would go to its full extent. Somewhere in the region of five feet of the fuse now ran out of the cairn of stones which he had built. At this point, Jack paused for a moment to consider what he was doing.

He ran over his ideas again, seeking any flaw in the reasoning. He could see none. The workers were all a mile or so from this point and would not be endangered by his action. If he was successful in bringing down this whole section of the cliff face, then clearing it away would be an enormous undertaking;

perhaps beyond the abilities of the crew who were laying the tracks which even now were snaking towards his home. The worst thing that could happen, at least as far as Jack McAndrew knew, was that the explosion would not have the desired effect and that it would just end up being a glorified firework of the sort that he and his brother had improvised from time to time when they were kids.

Well, there was no point in hanging round here debating the matter with himself any longer. Before actually setting fire to the fuse, the youngster went over to what he gauged the best spot for scrambling out of the chasm. He surely did not wish to be caught in here when that charge was detonated! Added to which, he had little or no idea how quickly that fuse would burn up. Looking at the way out of the crevice, Jack McAndrew calculated, based upon his wide experience of climbing in these mountains almost as soon as he could walk, that it would take him no more than a minute, two at the most to get clear of the place.

Even though he was sure that he was doing the right thing, Jack McAndrew's hands shook a little as he fumbled with the tinderbox. It took him six goes to get a spark from the flint, but, as soon as he did, the fuse began fizzing and sputtering in a most vigorous way. He bolted as fast as his legs would carry him.

CHAPTER 7

Don Rutledge was still trying to make up his mind about the wisdom, or otherwise, of riding up to the farmhouse and bracing the young fellow who lived there and warning him not to tangle with the Rocky Mountains Railroad Company. As usual, when he was feeling weak and undecided, he chose to take out his vexation on those around him. He shouted at the nearest men, 'Come on, you lazy bastards! Get a damned move on. You're like a bunch of old women.' From high overhead came a dull boom, which put Rutledge strongly in mind of the crack of artillery which he had heard so often during the war. But that made no sense at all; why would anybody be firing cannon up in those mountains? Then he watched in slowly fading disbelief as a section of the cliff-face some quarter of a mile long seemed to detach itself and begin moving towards him. It was such a peculiar and unexpected thing to see, that for a moment, Rutledge simply could not accept the incontrovertible evidence of his senses.

At the last moment, when he had less than a second of life remaining to him, the reality of his predicament dawned on Don Rutledge and he muttered, 'Oh, shit!' So it was that he was overtaken by eternity with a curse-word upon his lips.

The cliff had been perhaps more finely balanced than Jack's father had known when he promised his son that it would not fall for a thousand years or so. Rainwater had been seeping into a million cracks every winter and then freezing, the expansion of the ice widening every fissure, year after year. All that had been needed to bring down the entire cliff face had been that little nudge from the explosion set off by a reckless youth. Hundreds, perhaps thousands of tons of rock came crashing down onto the men working to set up the tents. Every last one of them was buried beneath the rock fall.

A mile and a half away, the men toiling on the railroad felt a sudden and inexplicable shudder as the ground shook beneath their feet. Some of them were from San Francisco and knew the premonitory signs of an earth tremor. Then there came a roaring, as of a distant freight train, combined with an unearthly rumbling. They looked up apprehensively to see the most extraordinary sight that any of them had ever seen in their lives: a vast column of dust was rising slowly from the valley ahead of them. It appeared to be as wide at its base as the mountain pass itself. As it rose into the still air, the cloud began to billow out until it spread across a greater area than the pass itself. This happened naturally, as when it reached the tops of the cliffs lining the pass, there nothing preventing its dissipation.

Clarence Harper was talking to Goldman when the ground shook beneath their feet. 'God almighty,' growled Harper, 'What in tarnation was that? Earthquake?'

The two men had their back to the pass and it was the excited jabbering of the coolies which caused them to turn around and see the cloud of dust billowing up at the entrance to the valley. 'Doesn't look like an earthquake,' remarked Goldman. 'Not any kind of earthquake I ever heard tell of, any ways.'

'Me neither. What d'you make of it?'

'I couldn't rightly say. You want I should ride out and see what's to do?'

'Yeah,' said Harper, 'That sounds like a good plan.' Inwardly, his heart was sinking as he could see at once that whatever had happened up at the pass looked likely to delay the operation in one way or another.

As he rode out towards the pass, Goldman was exulting. It was clear that something terrible had happened, maybe people killed. Was it too much to hope that Rutledge had been in the thick of whatever had occurred? Goldman didn't know much about geology, but, as he drew near, it looked to him as though there had been a rockfall or avalanche of some kind. It was hard to see through the dust, but from what he could make out, a large part of the cliffs at the entrance to the little valley had fallen down. As the scale of the destruction became clearer, he was torn between two conflicting feelings: on the one hand, the greater and more extensive the destruction, the more likely it was that Don Rutledge had met his death there; on the other hand though, if things were too bad, then it might make for serious delays in their schedule. Nobody knew better than Goldman how finely things were balanced in the race to the new port of Seattle, and a week's delay could make the difference between triumph and disaster. It would be no good having Rutledge out of the way and stepping into his shoes if the whole enterprise here fell to pieces. Where would be the profit in that?

By the time he reached the scene of the catastrophe, most of the dust had settled, leaving a clear view of the incredible situation. Hundreds of yards of the rocky cliffs had apparently collapsed. It took Goldman a moment to realize that there was no sign at all of the team of men who had come here to set up camp. Presumably, they had been buried beneath the rocks. Could it be that the same fate had befallen Rutledge?

There was still enough dust hanging in the air to make the view a little hazy. Abe Goldman looked up at the cliffs and, for a moment, could have sworn that he saw a figure standing there. It was hard to see properly with the dust swirling around. A speck of dirt landed in Goldman's eye and he blinked to remove it. When he looked up again, the man, if indeed there had really been anybody up there, had gone.

While he was peering uncertainly up at the mountains, Goldman heard the drumming of hoofs and turned to see a rider approaching from the valley. It was a grey-haired man with a seamed face. Not old, but definitely not young either. He reined in near Goldman and said, 'Hooey, that was one mighty crash. You weren't caught by it, I see.'

'No. No, I just got here.'

'My name's Jefferson. Habakkuk Jefferson.'

'Abe Goldman. I was working back there aways.'

'Ah,' said Jefferson, a look on his face which suggested that this information was not likely to increase his liking for Abe Goldman. 'One of the railroad men, is it? You folk are the devil of a nuisance, you know that?'

Goldman shrugged. 'We all got our jobs to do. What d'you suppose happened here?'

'It ain't hard to gauge. That whole cliff face was leaning over. Riddled with cracks and crevices. I guess it was just time for it to fall down.'

The magnitude of the disaster was beginning to sink in for Goldman. This was apt to mean the most

god-awful delay: it could spell the ruin of all his plans
to become a bigshot as Clarence Harper's right-hand
man. What would be the use of being the right-hand
man of a penniless bankrupt? He said hopefully, 'Say,
I don't suppose you've seen a bunch of fellows erecting tents anywhere hereabouts? Chinese, you know.'

'Nary a one,' said Habakkuk, with grim satisfac-
tion. 'If they were up this way, I'd say it was most like
they're buried under yonder rocks.'

'Yeah, that's what I thought.'

As the two men talked, three more riders came up
from the valley wondering if there was anything to be
done. They greeted Jefferson cheerfully and then
glared coldly at Goldman when Jefferson identified
him as an employee of the railroad company. It was
at this point that Clarence Harper rode up, desperately worried that something had ocurred which was
liable to hold up the progress of his railroad. He
went off to one side and talked for few moments in a
low voice with Abe Goldman. The other men dismounted and examined the rockfall, just on the off
chance that there might be somebody trapped whom
they could help. It did not escape notice that neither
of the men from the railroad seemed interested in
the possibility of rescuing their men.

It was a hopeless case. There was simply too much
rock for anybody anywhere near the cliff to have sur-
vived. Jefferson and the other farmers stood around
wondering if there was anything else they should be

doing to help.

After setting off the explosion, Jack McAndrew could hardly wait to see the consequences. He and his brother had fooled around with enough little bombs to make the young man childishly excited to see what he had wrought with that charge. It had been clear to him from the deafening roar and clouds of dust, that he had managed to bring down at least a portion of the cliff face, but he had no idea just how much. Would it be enough to prevent the railroad entering the valley? When he finally stood upon the newly formed edge to the cliffs and gazed down at the floor of the valley, he was awestruck at the extent of the devastation. 'Holy Moses!' he whispered, unable to believe that he had been solely responsible for the astonishing change in the topography of that part of McAndrew's Pass which lay below.

None of the coolies labouring away at laying tracks felt inclined to leave their work and come out to the pass to investigate. It would most likely cost them their jobs, so they just continued working and waited to see what the future would bring; Clarence Harper and Abe Goldman were the only men from the railroad present at the rock fall. Little by little, other men came from the valley to survey the damage. These were hard-bitten types, all of whom carried iron as a matter of routine.

Neither Harper nor Goldman was armed, but they

didn't apprehend any danger. It was apparent by now that all the tents, the chuck wagon and a whole heap of equipment lay buried beneath tons of rock. Not to mention, of course, a number of horses and forty-one men.

'You reckon Rutledge is under that lot?' Harper asked Abe Goldman.

'Hard to say,' said the other man judiciously, 'He might be and then again he mightn't. Only thing is, if he ain't under there, I'd've thought that all that noise would've brought him running.'

'I was thinking the self-same thing myself,' said Harper, ' 'Til, if and when he turns up, you can consider yourself business manager. That suit you well enough?'

'Sure,' said Goldman, inwardly exulting. Then he glanced up the valley and saw to his dismay the young man approaching who had shot at him and Rutledge just recently. He said to his boss, 'Might have trouble.'

Jack McAndrews was on foot and did not look to be in any particular hurry. He sauntered along casually, looking about him with great interest. It was at this moment that Goldman realized that he had indeed seen this boy up on the cliff a little earlier. But what could that mean? Surely it was not possible that he had had anything to do with it?

The men from the valley greeted McAndrew soberly, aware of the terrible loss which he had lately

100

suffered. He smiled and nodded to them, making all the while for Harper and Goldman. When he reached them, he said without any preamble, 'I know you two. I run one o' you off here and shot at the other. What are you doing up here?'

'This isn't your land, leastways not by my reckoning,' said Harper, 'or do you say it is?'

'No, my land begins a hundred yards up into the valley. This here is common land.'

'What do you want, boy?' asked Goldman, feeling that it was time to assert himself a little and show that he was now a person of some consequence since his recent promotion.

'What I *want* is to bring home my brother's murder to you, mister. I saw you there on that night when he was shot. I never looked to see you again so close to my own land.'

For a young man of such tender years, Jack spoke with great confidence. Since sending his mother off to safety, he had begun to grow into his new position of the man of the place, upon whom responsibility devolved for everything which happened on the farm.

Harper and Abe Goldman were uneasily aware that the other men from the valley had stopped talking and were watching carefully to see where this conversation might tend. 'You want to watch what you're saying, young man,' said Clarence Harper. 'Throwing round wild accusations is like to get you into trouble if you're not careful.'

Jack turned from Goldman to stare at the older man. 'Yes,' he said, 'I recognize you too. I ran you off my farm at the point of a gun, you recall? Come nigh to my land again and I'll do more than that next time.'

There was little purpose to be served in talking to such a hothead, so Harper and his new business manager decided that this was one of those times when, as the proverb tells us, discretion was very much the better part of valour. They chose to leave, rather than stay and bandy words with the young man. As they left, McAndrew called after them, 'You mind what I say, now. Show your faces on my land and I won't be answerable for what happens!'

It was not until the two men had left, that Jack learned that he had slaughtered over forty men that day. Another problem with youngsters is that they often have a callous streak in them which is worse than anything you might encounter in a body of more maturity and wisdom. Sure, he was sorry to hear about the men who had been killed, but this sorrow was not sufficiently great to mar his pleasure in having blocked the path of the railroad which had been heading their way.

As Harper and his newly appointed business manager rode back to where the coolies were still slaving away, Harper remarked, 'This is a damned nuisance and no mistake. We'll see what can be worked out about the route, but that boy'll have to go.' He shot a look at the man riding by his side and said, 'You understand what I'm talking about, right? When I say that the boy will have to go? You know that Rutledge was a real "stick-at-naught" in jobs like this?'

'I apprehend your meaning fully, Mr Harper,' replied Goldman coolly, 'You might recollect that it was I who killed that young fellow's brother. It ain't likely as I would hesitate to kill him as well.'

'Good man. I knew I was right about you. You look like a regular bookworm, but you got more sand than anybody I ever knew, bar your late lamented predecessor.'

So it was that as they got back to where the track was inching its way west, Abe Goldman knew that if he really wanted to be Harper's right hand man, he would have to go up to the pass at nightfall and kill the McAndrew boy.

After the other men had gone off about their business, Jack stood by the heaps of boulders and drifts of broken stone for a few minutes, thinking over what he had done. It was a fearful thing to kill a man, of that there can be no doubt, but burying forty men like this simply didn't seem like murder. It wasn't as though he'd stuck a knife in somebody, or pointed a gun at a man and pulled the trigger. All he had done was undertake a little blasting up in the mountains and if those men had chosen to come up to McAndrew's Pass poking around and preparing to invade the peace of the valley, well, all he could say is that it would have been better for them if they had not done so!

After these reflections, the youngster went back to the house and began cleaning and oiling both his pistol and scattergun. He thought of the Navy Colt as 'his' pistol now. After all, he had a better right to it than anybody else, or so he thought. After tapping out the wedge which held the barrel to the frame of the gun, he slid off the cylinder and began oiling the spindle. When he had finished, it spun as smoothly as a roulette wheel. Having made sure that the pistol was in good order, he turned his attention to the fowling piece, which he cleaned methodically before reloading. For such a young fellow, he had a good grasp of how things worked in this world, and he thought that unless he was very much mistaken, men would soon be coming to the house in order to kill him. What a mercy that he had arranged for his mother to be in a safe spot.

It was still only a little past midday and Jack didn't look for anybody to come meaning mischief in broad daylight. He figured that he might as well catch up on some of the chores that needed doing around the farm. It would be a shame for his mother to come home and find the place neglected, thus confirming all her reservations about leaving her son in charge.

To be on the safe side, the boy tucked the pistol in his belt before leaving the house. If he'd miscalculated the situation, then he didn't want to get caught with his pants down, as the saying went!

Harper had gathered together the foremen, who were all white, and the lone surveyor. Together with Abe Goldman, they all sat in a ring and tried to figure out how best to minimize the damage caused by the avalanche. Harper kicked off the proceedings by asking his surveyor, 'If we had to swerve round that heap of rock, could we do it without veering into the boggy part of the valley?'

'I'll have to go up there and see for myself,' said the surveyor, a man called Pete Logan. 'I'd say yes, from what you tell me. Only thing is—'

'Only thing is what?' asked Harper irritably, 'Don't tail off like that. You got something to say, then just out and say it.'

'I was going to say that if we curve round past that block, we can't just go straight back again on our original line. It'll take a mile or so after the rock fall to straighten up and get back to where we were heading.'

'Well,' said Harper pugnaciously, 'what of it?'

'It's nothing to me,' said Logan, 'but that would mean cutting clean through the fields around the farmhouse. It's one thing driving through rough pasture, but I'd think somebody'd have something to say if you run the tracks over fields of barley.'

'You let me worry about that. You ride out there this minute and bring me back a proper report. But as far as you can see, it would be possible?'

'If the owner of the farm don't object, sure it's possible.'

'Yeah, well,' said Harper, 'let's not worry overmuch about objections for now. Just get up there and see if you can swerve round the obstacle.'

Once Logan had left, Harper addressed the half-dozen foremen, saying, 'Those coolies can sleep out o' doors for a few nights, I suppose?'

'Reckon they'll have to,' said one of the men. 'Aint sure that I want to be doing the same. And what about food? Most of it's buried under half the mountain from all that I'm able to collect.' There were murmurs of agreement from the other men. Forcing coolies to sleep out under the stars was one thing, but expecting them to do the same was something else again.

'I'll tell you once and for all how things stand,' said Harper grimly. 'You boys are expecting bonuses once this line is finished. If it ain't finished, then there'll be no bonuses. More than that, there'll be no wages either for any man as is too delicate to sleep without a tent for a night or two. That's any man: Chinese, black or white, make's no odds to me. I'm sending back to Sawyer's Crossing and on to Fort Benton and hope to have something arranged soon, but until then, that's the situation. Those who don't like it can just leave.'

This was so uncompromisingly blunt that the men present knew that their boss wasn't fooling and that if they wished to retain their jobs, they would have to rough it for a space.

CHAPTER 8

Two things had happened by the time that the sun had set: the first was that the railroad tracks had crept within a half-mile of McAndrew's Pass and the other that Jack had left his house and was sitting quietly in the barn, setting a watch upon the surrounding countryside. He was positioned up in the hay-loft, right by a crack between the boards which gave him a perfect view along the valley towards Sawyer's Crossing. He could see the road leading to town and all the land in that direction. About a mile off, he could also see the lights of the cooking fires lit by the men working on the railroad.

Jack was not a surveyor, in fact his education had not extended far beyond reading, writing and simple arithmetic, but for all that, he was nobody's fool. He had already made his own calculations about the likely course of the railroad line, if it was forced to curve around the blockage he had caused. There were only two options: either it would have to veer south into the boggy ground, or it would have to pass right through his fields. Since the head of the whole undertaking had aready admitted that it would be impossible to lay the tracks across the soggy, swampy land, it meant that they would try to run through the farm. They had already had a good deal of trouble from him and his brother, making it most likely that somebody would be sent up here to make an end of him before work commenced in the morning.

It would be absurd to suggest that the youngster was not afraid for his life; he would hardly have been human otherwise. But his fear was not such as to paralyse him, or cause him to run away and hide in the mountains. He had told his mother that he could handle things if she went off to Fort Benton and that was just what he aimed to do.

It was a cloudless night and the moon was waning, but it was still only a few days past its fullest size, so the scene in front of Jack was lit up pretty well. It would hardly be possible for anybody to creep up to the house or barn without being seen. He reckoned that it would only be a single person coming to do him harm, two at most, which was a comforting thought. After all, how many assassins were likely to be working for a railroad company? Hardly more than one or two, he supposed. He wasn't sure how he would have tackled a whole band of killers. Mind, if it came to the matter of that, he wasn't overly keen on tackling even just the one.

By dusk, Don Rutledge hadn't shown up at the camp
and it was plain as could be to everybody that he
must have been killed. This meant that Goldman
could now congratulate himself upon having suc-
cessfully manoeuvred himself into the dead man's
shoes. It is, however, one thing to bend all your will
towards acquiring a thing and quite another to gain
enjoyment from the object of your desire when once
it is within your grasp. Abe Goldman had expended
so much energy intriguing and wriggling about like a
weasel in order to take over Rutledge's job, that now
he had it, he wasn't at all sure any more if it was what
he wanted. Being second-in-command of the Rocky
Mountains Railroad Company was all well and good;
nothing wrong at all with that aspect of the matter.
Going out at night with the intention of cold-
blooded murder though was something else again. It
was true that he had shot Tom McAndrew and not
been overwhelmed with remorse, but that had been
a confused, haphazard piece of business. Setting out
and saying to yourself, 'Well, I reckon I'm a' going to
kill a man tonight!', that was something else again.

There it was though. Clarence Harper had made it
clear that if he was to take over Rutledge's job, then
he had better be prepared to undertake all the duties
that the dead man had been happy to assume. One
of these was clearing the road of obstacles, using any

method which would accomplish that purpose. In the present case, that seemed to entail gunning down a stubborn boy.

As he thought about the projected murder, one of two things could have happened. Abe could have said to himself, 'The hell with it! I'm not a killer and I'm not going go off and shoot some kid with whom I have no quarrel.' The other choice would be that Goldman suppressed his finer feelings, shoved his conscience into a locked room and did as he had been bid in order to secure the job for which he had fought so hard. He sighed and went off to check that his pistol was in good order. Like many weak people, the moment when he turned bad passed quite naturally, without remark.

A little distance from the other men, Clarence Harper was walking up and down briskly, which he found helped him to think. One thing he knew for sure was that the entire enterprise was balanced upon the edge of a razor. The least deviation or error would spell the ruin of all his hopes. He might be able to browbeat the men to sleep without tents and make do on short commons for a couple of days more, but after that they would begin to slip away and he could forget about ever reaching the coast. They'd be off like rats from a sinking ship. Already, Harper was afraid that some of them had scented his fear, and once that happened, it was not long until you were altogether lost.

It was typical of the sort of person that Harper was, that never once did he think to blame himself for this current mess. He had cut corners, started work without establishing certain ownership of the land across which he would be passing, and taken any number of other shortcuts. In retrospect, it had been a matter of time before he ran up against somebody who would not be bullied or buffaloed into giving way. None of this occurred to him though. All he could think of was to put all the blame on that cocky young bastard up at McAndrew's Pass. It would ease his mind greatly when he knew that Goldman had settled that boy.

It was a strange thing, thought Jack, that at the very time when you know that you must not let yourself fall asleep, that is precisely when your eyelids become heavy and you find yourself yawning and longing for your bed. He shook his head and took a deep breath. It would help if he could move about a little; maybe jump up and down and wave his arms about. But it was life and death that he didn't take his eyes off the approach to the pass. If he started dozing now, why, some devil might put a ball through his brains while he slumbered and he would never wake again.

The moon had risen and was casting its ghastly pale light over the fields. As he watched, McAndrew was aware of a flicker of movement. He peered hard and saw that it was a man and that he was heading this way. From all that he could collect, the fellow was not making any kind of effort at concealment. He looked as though he was just taking a stroll through the countryside in the light of day. A doubt assailed Jack. Surely, this wasn't how a ruthless killer would come looking for him. Wouldn't such a one creep up secretively, hoping to catch him by surprise. This man was just walking along quite normally. He looked harder, wondering if it could be one of the farmers from up the valley who sometimes went down to Sawyer's Crossing. He couldn't make out the fellow's features in this light and at that distance; his face was only a little white blur. He would have to wait until the man drew closer.

There didn't, to Abe Goldman, seem much point in tiptoeing around in the dark and hoping to catch that young fellow unawares. It would make more sense to march up to his house, knock on the door and represent himself as having come in the role of emissary of peace. Perhaps he could tell the boy that he was hoping to find a compromise or something. Shit, it didn't matter what the story was. Then, when young McAndrew was offguard or turned his back on Goldman, he could shoot him. That would also avoid the unpleasant prospect of a gun battle or something of that nature.

As he got closer to the farmhouse, Goldman noticed that there didn't seem to be lights anywhere. Surely it was too early for the young man to be asleep in his bed. Then again, he didn't really know that much about life on farms. Maybe they got up at the crack of dawn and then retired at a ridiculously early hour. It would be a real nuisance if he had to knock on the door and rouse his intended victim from his bed. It would be likely to delay things as well. All that Goldman hoped was to deal with this little problem as expeditiously as could be and then get back to the camp.

As the figure drew closer, Jack saw that it was the man who had been up at the rock fall earlier. The same fellow who had been there when his brother was killed. Had this man actually pulled the trigger on that occasion? He didn't look the type. To McAndrew's eyes, he looked more like a clerk in a grocery store than he did a gunman. Very slowly and being careful to stay deep in the shadows so that no movement of his would be seen from below, the young man cocked both barrels of his scattergun and then stood up and took aim through the space between the boards forming the wall of the old barn. By now, the man walking into the yard between the house and barn was only twenty-five yards away. Jack could hit a squirrel in the eye at that range and he took first pull on the trigger.

Standing there in the yard, it seemed to Abe that there was no sign of life at all. Could the boy be out working the fields or something? Surely farmers stopped when it got dark, didn't they? Or maybe he really had gone to bed at dusk and was now sleeping like a babe. Well, he'd just knock on the door and take it from there.

Up in the barn, McAndrew took his finger off the trigger. He knew that he could not shoot a man from cover in this way without challenging him. It would put him on a par with the worst kind of cowardly ambush-killer. It was no good, he'd have to go and at least talk to him and see if he meant harm or not.

As he walked to the door of the farmhouse, Goldman was determined to show himself to be a peacable and well-intentioned citizen; a man hoping to smooth over past unpleasantness and help all parties avoid future trouble. There was a pistol at his hip, but he managed to convey by his demeanour that it was a rare occurrence for him to be carrying, which was at least true. When Jack McAndrew came up quietly behind him, holding a twelve-gauge shotgun at the ready, Goldman was able to display unfeigned shock and amazement in a most convincing and true-to-life fashion. He really didn't need to act.

'Hey fella,' he said nervously, when he heard a sound behind him and turned swiftly to see what it was, 'there's no need at all for firearms. I'm a man of peace.'

'You're carryin',' pointed out the young man, 'I can see a gun at your hip this minute.'

'Oh, that?' said Goldman, like he'd forgotten it

was there. 'My boss likes us to have weapons with us when we go off at night. Lord knows why.'

'What do you want?' enquired Jack pertinently, 'I'll warrant you ain't come here this time o' night for to make a social call.'

'You got that right!' said the other with a nervous chuckle. 'You about to put up your gun and stop aiming it at me?'

The youngster, who was holding the scattergun low with the butt resting on his hip, said, 'No, I don't believe that I will. Not 'til you give me a good account o' what you're doing here an' what you're after. You were there when my brother was killed. You shoot him?'

Goldman felt as though a chilly hand had gripped his heart and for a moment he couldn't breathe. If the boy had it in his head that he had shot his brother, then it was all up with him. The lawyer managed at last to get out a few words. 'Lord, no. That was the fellow I was with, name of Rutledge. Don Rutledge. If you're seeking vengance of him though, you're a mite too late. He died this morning when that cliff fell down.'

There could be truth in this, thought Jack McAndrew. Then again, it didn't explain what this shifty-looking little fellow had been doing up at the farm the night Tom died. McAndrew recollected the keg of gunpowder. Was this man claiming that he hadn't known what was afoot when he came up to the house with that other man?

The silence, combined with the fact that Jack showed no inclination to lower his weapon, was having a very bad effect on Goldman. This was not at all how he had thought things would turn out. At length, he said, 'What's on your mind, son?' He thought that a friendly, fatherly tone of voice might meet the occasion, but he had misjudged the youngster standing in front of him. Goldman's attempt at being paternal rang quite false and only served to give Jack cause to think that the other man was hoping to deceive him.

After a pause of thirty seconds or so, McAndrew said, 'Do you stand there and tell me now that you and your partner meant my family no harm that night? Which of you was carrying a ten-pound keg of powder?'

The question was so unexpected that Goldman felt himself flushing and was, for the moment, wholly lost for words. The boy observed all this narrowly and said slowly, 'Yes, it's just as I figured. The two of you were in it up to your ears. You come up here to kill me and my family. What was you plannin'? To spring a mine outside the house and then shoot us down when we came running out?'

This was so close to the mark that Goldman was once again lost for words. He wondered momentarily if he should at this point go for his gun, but the young man standing in front of him already had the

117

drop on him with the shotgun. It would be madness to try anything. Goldman said, 'Sounds like you have me all tried and convicted. It's not in reason that you are in a mood to listen to anything I've got to say. What are you aiming to do? Just shoot me down?'

For one so young, Jack McAndrew had a way with him since his brother's death and the departure of his mother that made him seem a good deal older than his years. He spoke like a full-grown and very confident man, rather than a green youth. 'It'd be no more than you deserve. I don't know which o' you two pulled the trigger that night, but it's plain as a pikestaff that you both meant to kill me and my mother and brother. I ought to shoot you down right now.'

At the realization that he was not about to be killed on the spot, Abe Goldman felt weak with relief. What did the boy have in mind instead? Handing Goldman over to the sheriff of Sawyer's Crossing? Well that would be just fine and dandy, because Mort Williams knew how things were placed and he wouldn't expect to be detained too long by that weak-willed individual. 'So what's it to be then?' he asked, 'You making a citizen's arrest or something, on suspicion of murder?'

'Citizen's arrest?' asked McAndrew, surprised. 'I don't know anything about that. No, what I'm thinking is you and me settle the matter here and now. Just the two of us.'

118

As the meaning of the young man's words sank in, Abe had a sudden and overpowering urge to make water. Then he thought that he might have misunderstood and be taking too pessimistic view of the case. Perhaps he would yet escape with no more than a few bruises. He said, 'What do you mean, a fist fight between you and me? Well, it's hardly fair, after all you're younger and tougher than me. Still, if that's what you'll have.'

'Fist fight? I ain't talkin' 'bout no fist fight. We ain't in the schoolyard. You came up here just lately looking to kill me and my whole family; now I'm offering you the chance to kill me. Only this time, it'll be on equal terms.'

'But. . . .' Goldman struggled for words, a rare sensation for the lawyer, for whom easy words were a stock-in-trade. 'But that's crazy. Just plumb crazy. I'm not a gunfighter. You can't mean that we are to fight with pistols?'

'You came up here carryin' a gun for the Lord night. I'm offering you the chance to do it, fair and square.'

As though he was in a dream, Goldman watched the young man in front of him bend down slowly, although never once taking his eyes from Goldman, and gently place his scattergun on the ground. Then he stood up straight and flipped aside his jacket to reveal the pistol tucked carelessly in his belt. 'Here's how we'll play it,' he said to Goldman. 'We'll both of us move back for five paces. Then you can count to three and then we'll fire. Gives you an edge.'

Abe Goldman could still scarcely believe that this was happening to him. For the merest fraction of a second, he considered whipping out his pistol and trying to take this preternaturally self-assured and calm young man by surprise and killing him while he was still setting out the rules for the preposterous duel. What stopped him was not that this would have been a cowardly and treacherous action, but rather that young McAndrew never once took his eyes off him and Goldman had, in any case, the uncomfortable notion that he was expecting such a move.

There was no time to consider anything else though, because the McAndrew boy was standing there waiting for him to begin. And still, Goldman couldn't quite bring himself to believe that all this was real and that he was about to fight for his very life.

'Ready?' asked Jack and took one step backwards. Automatically, Goldman did the same. Then the two of them took another step back. It put Goldman in mind of some children's game: grandmother's footsteps, perhaps. Then they repeated the process and did so twice more, until they were maybe fifteen or twenty feet from each other.

His heart was pounding as though it would burst out of his chest and he found that his breathing was also laboured. Goldman stood there in the moonlight, staring stupidly at Jack. McAndrew said, 'What you waitin' for? Why'nt you count to three and be done with it?'

Goldman's voice was thick with dread and sounded, to his own ears at least, distorted and far away, like he was under water or something. He said, 'One.'

There was a longish pause, before he could bring himself to say, 'Two.' For the life of him, he could not make his lips form the word 'Three'. He gulped and swallowed, bringing saliva into his mouth to moisten his lips and tongue. 'Three!' he declared.

Somehow, Goldman thought that pronouncing that fateful word would in itself be enough to precipitate a blur of deadly motion and the roar of gunfire. But he hadn't gone for his gun when he said 'Three' and the youngster showed no sign of going for his either. Then McAndrew said, 'Ain't you goin' to fire? 'Cause if you ain't, I surely am!'

And then there was nothing at all for it but to try and kill the young man taunting him. Abe snatched at the pistol hanging at his hip and his fingers were round the hilts, the weapon moving free of the holster, when there came a crash like thunder and Goldman knew that he hadn't been quick enough. He didn't at first feel the shock of the ball driving through his chest. All that happened was that he found himself tilting first one way and then another; suddenly giddy and unable to stand up straight. Then he knew that he had been shot and thought

121

that he should try and fire back. His hand though felt too heavy to lift and so, instead, he stood there fool-ishly, unable to move. A second later, Goldman tumbled to the ground in a heap, the pistol slipping from his nerveless fingers. As he lay there, con-sciousness slipping away, Jack came over and stood right over him, looking down at the man he had shot. He said, 'All I got to do now is go after your boss.'

CHAPTER 9

All Clarence Harper's hopes began to evaporate like the morning dew as he rose the next day. It had been some good long while since Harper had slept out under the stars and it was not an experience that he was anxious to repeat. He felt various aches and pains and wanted nothing so much as to have a long soak in a hot bath. There being no prospect of such a thing right then, he thought that he might as well get up and go and bully somebody instead; this always cheered him a little.

It was when he had opened his eyes, stood up and began walking around that Harper knew that he was ruined. The Chinese workers who, in the usual way of things, put up with all sorts of treatment which the regular white workers would not endure, had had enough. Being told that they would have to do without shelter for the foreseeable future was the last straw. The men whom Harper had set over them were an unpleasant crew and had been harrying and urging the men on in ways that would not have come amiss in a Southern plantation before the war. This had caused discontent already and the loss of the tents and chuck wagon was unendurable.

There was no work at all being done, although the sun had been up for some time. A steady stream of men was heading back east in the general direction of Sawyer's Crossing, their packs on their backs. The foremen shouted and raved, but, being greatly out-numbered, did not attempt to lay hands on anybody. Those who were not already walking away were busily packing up their things. It was clear that in another hour there would be no workers left to lay any more tracks. The Rocky Mountains Railroad was finished.

'What's the game?' Harper enquired angrily of one of the foremen, a tough and capable fellow who was known to lash out with his fists if he felt that any of the coolies weren't showing him the proper amount of respect.

'Nothing to be done, sir,' the man told him. 'It's not just a few. Every man-Jack of 'em is leaving. Short of shooting a few, I don't see as we can stop them.'

'You think that would do the trick?' asked Harper hopefully.

The man looked sharply at his boss and said, 'Like enough they'd fall upon us and tear us to pieces. There's a whole lot of them and only a few of us.'

'I dare say you're right,' said Harper. 'What would

you say are the chance of recruiting any workers from Sawyer's Crossing?'

'Really? I'd say next door to zero. Once those boys hit town with their stories, I don't see anybody coming out here to rough it without even a tent or proper food.'

Something occurred to Harper and he said, 'Where's Abe Goldman? He might have some ideas as'd be some use, 'stead of can't do this and won't do the other. There's a man who brings me solutions, not problems.'

The foreman, whose name was Martin Cole, said, 'He went up to the pass last night and didn't come back yet.'

'Not back yet? What are you talking about?'

'Just as I say,' Cole replied stolidly. 'I thought you knowed 'bout it, begging your pardon.'

'Knew he was going up to McAndrew's Pass, didn't know he hadn't come back though.'

Cole looked at his boss oddly and then said, in a neutral and disinterested voice, making it plain that he wasn't poking his nose into matters which did not concern him, 'There was a single shot heard. Sounded like a pistol. Came from up that way. Nothin' more though.'

'What about you?' said Harper. 'You going to light out as well as those Chinese?'

Martin Cole shrugged. 'Long as you pay me, I'll carry on working for you, sir. But there's only a half-dozen of us, just me and the other men as was in charge o' them coolies. I doubt we'll be able to build the railroad by our own selves.'

Without speaking further to the man, Harper turned on his heel and went off to see if anything could be salvaged from the wreckage of his dreams. If only he hadn't been in such a damned hurry and had allowed the surveyors more time to make sure of what they were about. But he had always been urging them on and encouraging them to cut corners. And it had worked! By threats, violence and spirited legal action, he had succeeded in riding roughshod over anything and everybody in his way. Why, the speed that his crew had made up to this point was purely amazing. Had he only been able to maintain it, he and his railroad line would have gone down in history as the quickest laying of a line in American history.

History, however, tends to concern itself with the story of winners: those who come out on top. The name of the first company to complete a line running across to the North Pacific coast would be remembered; those who came second or, as seemed all too likely in the present case, failed entirely to finish the course, would be forgotten. It was a bitter thought.

It is a melancholy fact that no matter how bad things are they can always get worse. Clarence Harper was to learn this truth before the sun set. He tried to talk to one or two of the coolies, but they showed no inclination to linger and simply muttered politely and incomprehensibly at him, before dodging to one side and making off towards Sawyer's Crossing. His foremen stood around looking helpless and also not inconsiderably vexed. They had presumably by this time worked out that their jobs too were most probably at an end. None of them showed much desire to meet Harper's eye and he guessed that once the last of the coolies had gone, those men would not be far behind.

It was a stroke of luck for Harper that the rider came down from the pass before all his men had deserted him. Three of the foremen were huddled together talking, perhaps wondering if they would get paid for their day's work. The others were still trying to chivvy some of the coolies into staying. It was a hopeless task. The Chinese would not argue openly, but as soon as everybody's back was turned, they slipped off quietly. Despite all this, the white men whose job it was to supervise the navigators and get the greatest possible amount of work out of them were still present and, at least for now, beholden to Harper and prepared to stick with him until he discharged them.

Harper watched the approaching horseman, hope rising in his breast for a moment that it might be Abe Goldman, with some wonderful scheme to rescue his fortunes. Then, as the rider drew near, he realized that it was the McAndrew boy, which meant that the likelihood was that he needn't expect to see Goldman again in this world. The foremen were staring at the boy too as he came on. When once he was within hailing distance, Harper said, 'Well, what will you have?'

'I told you and your hired man not to come on my land. You recollect?'

'Listen, boy,' said Harper, any patience with which he had once been blessed eroded into nothing by the morning's events. 'I don't know that I have anything to say to you. This land doesn't belong to you. Anybody trespassing, I reckon it's you.'

Jack cast his eye around the camp, noting that it was all but deserted and that the last few men were even now making off in the general direction of Sawyer's Crossing. 'Having some trouble? Don't look to me like I'm going to be worrying any more about your railroad line crossing my land. I'm glad.'

'What do you want?' asked Harper shortly.

'You and me got business to discuss. But just the two of us.'

'Get on out of here! I got nothing to say to you. Keep your damned hovel and that dirt-box you call a farm. You can see for yourself, nobody's like to lay any tracks your way. Leastways,' Harper hastily amended, hopeful of the future still, 'not for a while, anyways.'

'You stayin' here?'

128

'That's no affair of yours. I got naught else to say to you.'

The young man looked round and saw clearly that if he made any move on the railroad boss here and now, then those half-dozen men standing around watching would be very likely to intervene. He'd leave it for now and hope to catch Harper on his own later. He nodded amiably, touched the brim of his hat and turned his horse around, trotting off back the way he had come.

Martin Cole came over to where Harper was staring after the departing rider and said, 'What in the hell was all that about?'

'I guess he came by to tell me that Abe Goldman is dead.'

Cole gave his boss a look. Harper didn't seem disposed to say anything more and so the foreman went back to the other men, who were still wrangling over whether there was any purpose in staying with Harper or if he was now a busted flush. It went without saying that if Clarence Harper was still a wealthy businessman, then it was worth sticking to him and helping sort out this temporary difficulty for him. That would bring rewards in the future. If, on the other hand, he was ruined financially by the events of the last day or two, then they might as well dig up. Only Don Rutledge and Abe Goldman had had any idea just how close to the wind Harper had been sailing with this whole project and the men standing about now, talking things over, could not really bring themselves to believe that the boss was through. Surely he would just need to buy more tents and food and then hire more labourers?

It might have been thought that killing Goldman would have satisfied young Jack McAndrew's thirst for vengeance, but it had on the contrary only whetted his appetite. Since Tom's death, Jack had hardened a great deal knowing that he was now the man of the place and responsible for taking care of his mother. More than that, the loss of his brother had become sharper with the passage of time. He had somehow expected the pain to be dulled as the days passed, but quite the opposite happened. As he rode away from Harper that morning, Jack knew that the only way to settle this business, so that he could get on with his life, would be to make an end to the man who was ultimately responsible for wrecking his family.

There was not only the death of his brother to be counted in the reckoning, but also the breaking of his mother's heart. Jenny McAndrew had always been a strong and resilient woman, who had raised her sons and kept the farm going, even after her husband had been killed in the war. As far back as he could remember, Jack had always known his mother as tough and indomitable; someone who could handle anything which life threw at her. When she had gone off in old Habakkuk Jefferson's wagon though, she had been a shadow of her former self. All the vim and vigour had drained out of her and she was like a silent ghost. This was worse even than seeing his brother killed, having his mother's personality altered so.

So it was that even as he had turned the mare and left Harper and his men, Jack had known that it would not end there and that if he had revenged himself yesterday on the two men who had killed his brother, then he still had not yet had his vengeance on the man whose machinations had resulted in the breaking of his mother's spirit.

After young McAndrew left, Clarence Harper felt distinctly uneasy. It was ridiculous; as if he didn't have enough to worry about, without giving thought to that crazy boy! Harper had one last string in his bow and that was that the men he had despatched to Fort Benton would be able to lay hands upon tents, a new chuck wagon and so on. If he could, by offering an increase on what he had been paying the coolies, manage to recruit a gang of men in Sawyer's Crossing, he might still pull through. Because the alternative was too dreadful to contemplate, he put all his energy into this means of pulling himself out of the hole into which he feared he was slithering.

'Cole and you others,' Harper barked, as soon as Jack McAndrew had left, 'here's the way of it. I still want you men and if you stay with me, your wages are secure. We're going back to Sawyer's Crossing and we're going to do our damnedest to get some men to work up here. Even if they'll only come for a week or two, that'll be enough.'

'They won't stay 'less you can provide proper shelter and food,' said Martin Cole. 'Those coolies will have spread the word by the time we get to town – about some of our mishaps, that is.'

'I want one of you men to ride as fast as you can to Fort Benton. Find out what's going on there. The rest of us are bound for Sawyer's Crossing. See if you can speed things up in Fort Benton and get tents and food to arrive here. We'll still make it, see if we don't.'

Mort Williams cursed the day that he had ever had any dealings with the Rocky Mountains Railroad Company. Being handed $500 like that had seemed at the time like a gift from the gods. Now, he believed that it must have come from the Devil himself, the amount of trouble that money had brought to him.

After freeing Don Rutledge, the sheriff assumed that once the railroad company had moved on up to McAndrew's Pass, then he would never need give them another thought. Sure, that boy turning up had caused him to be anxious, but that episode too had faded away and three days after the line had forged on past his town, Mort Williams was congratulating himself on having had a narrow escape; as the saying goes, 'All's well that ends well'. It was then that two men had ridden into Sawyer's Crossing, asking about the dead stranger.

By the time questions were being asked, the unfortunate man killed by Rutledge had been dead and buried for forty-eight hours. He had paid for a room for the night in a boarding house and his bags contained no clues about his identity or occupation. There was just a thick ledger, filled with copious notes in a tiny and barely legible hand. There was also a file of cuttings from newspapers, which chiefly concerned a company of which Williams had never heard, called Credit Mobiliere. Whoever the man was, he was clearly literate and perhaps better educated than most of the types who hung around the Tanglefoot.

There had been sufficient money on the body to pay for a funeral, which Sheriff Williams had felt duty bound to attend. He had been the only mourner; nobody else in town knew anything of the man who had just turned up and spent that one, ill-fated evening in the saloon, which had culminated in his death. His books and other meagre belongings, the sheriff stored in his office, on the remote chance that somebody came looking for the fellow.

The two men who turned up at the sheriff's office were shrewd-looking types who described the dead man to a 'T' and made it plain that they knew he had arrived in Sawyer's Crossing and hadn't been heard of since. Mort Willaims thought about it and decided that the story of the death was known to too many for him to be able to conceal it from these inquisitive strangers. He said, 'Yes, I mind that somebody fitting that description met an unfortunate accident here, a few days since.'

'How's that?' said one of the men, right sharp and quick, like he suspected some funny business, 'Accident you say? What kind of accident?'

'He got into a fight and came off worse. Fact is, he died of it.'

The second man, who was more softly spoken than his companion and gave the impression of being pretty well educated, said, 'Our friend was fond of a drink, as nobody can deny. And I'd be deceiving you, Sheriff, if I were not to tell you straight that he'd been in fights before. But it is what you might term a curious coincidence that he should have died here, so soon after coming to your town.'

'Coincidence, you say?' said Williams slowly, an awful foreboding gripping him. 'What kind o' coincidence?'

'May we speak plainly, Sheriff?'

'Might be for the best,' said the sheriff, wondering whether his freeing that wretch Rutledge from gaol was likely to bring down trouble upon his head now.

'Well then, it's like this. We, which is to say this gentleman and I, work for a newspaper back East. It's called the *New York Times*. You ever hear of it?'

Mort Williams, who wasn't much of a one for reading, shook his head.

'Our colleague, David Sykes, who from what you say may no longer be with us, was delving a little here, looking into a story which could be explosive. I say explosive advisedly, touching as it does upon various well regarded persons in Congress and certain big wheels in the world of banking. By the way, do you have any personal effects of this fellow you buried? They might prove the case one way or another.'

It was on the tip of Sheriff Williams' tongue to deny all knowledge of any effects, but he had the uncomfortable feeling that these two characters were tenacious as bloodhounds and the quicker he gave them what they wanted, the more likely he was to be rid of them in a hurry. He accordingly went over to a cupboard and unlocked it. Then he removed the thick book and the file of cuttings. He said, 'Fellow didn't have a whole heap o' cash on him and what he did have just 'bout paid for his funeral. Spare clothes went to the minister, who's give 'em to the poor and needy by now. All that remained was these.'

There could be no doubt, after seeing the eager, almost greedy, way that the two men scanned the miniscule writing of the ledger-book, that the dead man had indeed been known to them and had left something valuable behind; although what all that tiny writing crammed onto each page of the book might signify was more than Mort Williams could say. Fact was it meant something to them. After they had looked through the book for a bit, one of them glanced up and asked, 'Would you happen to know where Mr Clarence Harper is currently to be found? Is he still with the crew building this new railroad of his?'

'I believe so.'

'Then we needn't trouble you any further, Sheriff. Oh, there is just one small point: did you lay hands on the man responsible for Mr Sykes's death?'

CHAPTER 10

Having decided that the only thing that would now satisfy him would be the death of Clarence Harper, the head of the whole railroad enterprise, young Jack McAndrew found himself curiously reluctant to set off in pursuit of his victim, who, he assumed, would be heading by now to Sawyer's Crossing. He pottered about the house, tidying and cleaning, so that when his mother returned the place would not resemble a pig-pen; all the while, his mind worked fast. He was certainly not afraid of shooting another man: he now knew that he had killed a considerable number of men in the last few days, including one whom he had shot at a distance of less than twenty feet. There was no doubt but that he was capable of murder. He had slung the body of Abe Goldman over his horse and taken it up to the site of the rock fall, where he'd dumped it and then laid a few rocks over it, suggesting that it was just one more victim of the tragic accident there. He guessed that by the time anybody started looking closely, the body would be so decayed that nobody would spot the bullet wound. Most likely all the corpses beneath those rocks had holes and gashes of varying sizes.

The doubts and anxieties which were besetting Jack were not that he might be unable to kill Harper, but rather of the practical and ethical aspects of the matter. On a practical level, killing the man in town might end up with him in gaol, even facing trial and execution. Mort Williams, the sheriff, was clearly in the pocket of the railroad men and would most likely take their side in any dispute. Even if he killed Clarence Harper in a fair duel, might not the sheriff treat it as cold-blooded murder?

This alone would not perhaps have been enough to deter the hot-headed youngster, but how would it affect his mother if she faced the loss of her other son? And who would there then be to protect his ma and run the farm? This needed serious thought. It would be crazy to carry out a killing on his mother's behalf if the consequence was that she was worse off afterwards than she was before!

It would be stretching the case to say that Jack had an elaborate code of ethics by which he lived his life, but there were certain inflexible rules that he could not think of violating. One of these was the use of lethal force against an unarmed man. He just knew that this was plain wrong and not a thing that any decent and honourable man would ever consider. Fact was, he hadn't seen that railroad boss wearing a gun at all. Bigshot businessman like that, chances were he never did carry iron. McAndrew knew very well that whatever he had found himself to be capable of in recent days, he could never gun down an unarmed man.

It was accordingly with a troubled heart and uncertain mind that he set off for Sawyer's Crossing later that day.

Meanwhile, in Sawyer's Crossing itself, the two journalists from the *New York Times* who were investigating the worst case of corruption anybody could recall, the Credit Mobiliere scandal, had learned that it was common knowledge that the business manager of the Rocky Mountains Railroad Company had provoked a quarrel with their colleague and then killed him. This was too much of a coincidence for their taste and they were both of them convinced, quite erroneously, that David Sykes had been deliberately silenced on the orders of one of the principal figures in the Credit Mobiliere affair. The question was, how to bring this death home to Clarence Harper? The first arrests for bribery and corruption were, according to their sources, due to take place in New York and Washington within a matter of days. And here they were, out in the middle of nowhere, with one of the prime movers of the business within touching distance. Why, it would be the story of the decade if they were able to see Harper himself arrested, and not only for crooked business practices, but for complicity in murder!

Mort Williams was a weak-willed and venial man, who was also as changeable as a weathercock. The two men from the newspaper back East struck him as being very sure of themselves and if the half of what they had said was true, then he could be in big trouble. How was he to know that the owner of the railroad company was a crook? One row in the Tanglefoot was much the same as another and now he was being told that this particular fight had been staged and was in fact in the nature of an assassination, with the chosen victim being a journalist from this important New York newspaper. And he had let the murderer walk free!

The sheriff had made a decision since learning all these disturbing facts, which was that he might very well be in hot water for something over the next week or two. The only real question was what would be the easier option, assuming that he was going to land in trouble. Would it be the fact that he had accepted what was tantamount to a bribe from a man who was, from all that he was able to collect, a notorious crook? Or would it be worse to be in the frame for a conspiracy involving a murder and allowing a wanted killer to go free? As Mort Williams saw it, there was no question but that he would sooner be thought of as a man who had taken a corrupt payment, rather than one who had been involved in covering up a murder. That being so, Williams figured that the best way out of the trap in which he found himself would probably be to ignore the threats of his having taken that $500 and gambled it away coming to light, and to crack down right hard on the men who had planned to assassinate the jounalist in the saloon not so long ago.

The more Williams thought about it, the better this scheme appeared to be. If these men were as corrupt and crooked as he was being led to believe, then it would be his word against theirs if any accusations were to be bandied about. Besides, if he arrested that Abe Goldman and his boss, he could search their belongings and maybe there he would find the recipt he had signed and which had been held over his head as likely to bring about his ruin. By the evening, Sheriff Williams had sworn in three men who sometimes acted as deputies when there was need, and was getting ready to move in on the head of the Rocky Mountains Railroad Company. With luck, he would come out as the hero of the piece and get his name in the newspapers as the man who caught the biggest swindler ever heard of in the United States.

At first, Mort Williams's plan had been to ride out to McAndrew's Pass and catch up with Clarence Harper and his chief assistants there, but around midday, he heard that they had returned to town.

The sheriff didn't know what was happening, because all his workers had also fetched up in Sawyer's Crossing. Clearly, something was in the wind.

'You, Cole,' said Harper, once they reached town, 'Take another man and ask around about getting more men to work up at the pass. Make it clear that it's only two weeks' work and that we're paying well. We'll come out on top of this yet, you'll see.' Privately, Martin Cole had his doubts about this, but went off to do the boss's bidding anyway.

The day wore on until it reached about five. By that time, Mort Williams and his three temporary deputies were assembled in the sheriff's office. Williams explained what needed to be done before darkness. He said, 'Here's how things stand, boys. You all thought that Harper was a big financier and I don't know what all else. Well, he ain't. I have it on the best authority that he's like a damned corkscrew in his business dealings and that it's all up with him. Word is, he's like to be arrested for embezzlement directly.'

None of the three men liked to remind the sheriff that he had seemed to be the best friend of the railroad men until a few hours ago. The story of how he had released a man who had committed homicide in front of twenty witnesses had been all over the town for days.

'Anyways,' continued Williams, 'here's how the

case stands now. I am aiming to take in two of Harper's men. That would be a fellow called Goldman and another whose name is Rutledge. I made a mistake letting that Rutledge go after the death in the Tanglefoot, which I freely admit.'

'What about this Goldman?' asked one of the men. 'What is he wanted for?'

'Corruptly offering an inducement to a peace officer with a view to interfering in his duty,' said Mort Williams promptly. 'That's a serious matter and I'll be charging 'em both, most likely, and sending them to Coulson for trial.'

'What about Mr Harper?'

Sheriff Williams stopped to think about this for a bit and then said, 'If Harper doesn't interfere with our investigations, then all well and good. If he does, then maybe we'll have to hold him as well.'

The deputies all understood that something had happened to change the state of play as regards the Rocky Mountains Railroad Company. The day before, everybody was treating those men like they were the next door to being untouchable; now, they were going to arrest them. Not only that, but throughout the day a trickle and then a flood of coolies had been turning up in town. Construction of the railroad line had evidently come to a halt. None of the three men enlisted by Williams was bothered about this, or even especially curious; they were being paid and that was all that mattered to them.

'Anyways,' said Mort, 'we're going to have another pot o' coffee and then we going after 'em.'

By the time Jack reached town, he was still undecided about the best course of action. The two men who had been there when his brother Tom was killed, had died themselves at his own hands. Maybe that was enough. If he went after Harper here in Sawyer's Crossing, then his mother was apt to lose the second of her sons, one way or another and he couldn't see how that would be a kindness to her. It was a real conundrum. On the one hand, the young man felt that Harper was ultimately to blame for Tom's death and should be made to pay for it. On the other, he was reluctant to make things worse for his Ma.

When he hit town, McAndrew tethered his horse and then wandered disconsolately along Main Street, his mind working furiously, the desire for vengeance contending with a wish not to expose his mother to further unpleasantness. Although he was not a drinker, the youngster felt like some human company and so thought he'd visit the Tanglefoot saloon. He didn't, after all, have to have any intoxicating liquor there. Surely they'd be glad enough to serve him some soda or something.

At a table right at the back of the bar-room, sat Clarence Harper with four of his men. They understood that they were still being paid and that there was, at least according to the boss, no prospect of their being out of work just yet awhiles. All they were called upon to do now was to sit drinking from the bottle of whiskey which Harper had caused to be delivered to their table and to listen to what their boss had to say.

'You boys might have heard,' said Harper expansively, 'that it was me and a few others who transformed the Union Pacific line from a dream to a reality. Yes, sir, there are those who dream and those who roll up their sleeves and get to work. Me, I never been a dreamer. I am a doer, that's what I am!'

Harper had his back to the room, else he would have seen what the four other men at the table saw: the sheriff of Sawyer's Crossing, accompanied by three heavily armed men, enter the Tanglefoot and make a beeline for them. It was obvious that something untoward was afoot, because the sheriff had a rifle tucked under his arm and one of the men with him was cradling a sawn-off scattergun. All four of the men sitting at the table with Harper were carrying iron. They were none of them gunmen or anything of the sort, but at the same time, not one of them was the sort of man to allow himself to be bossed about without good cause. Unless the sheriff was about to show considerably more diplomatic skill than was usual with him, it was not hard to predict that there was likely to be some degree of unpleasantness on the horizon.

The Tanglefoot was almost empty, so when Jack

entered the place, it only took a quick look around the bar before he saw Harper sitting at a table towards the back of the room. He had his profile to McAndrew as he walked through the batwings and the sight of the man who had been so much on his mind, drove all thoughts of drinking from the boy's head. He slowed right down and just stood there for a moment by the bar, staring across at the table where the man responsible for his brother's death and his mother's grief, looked to be holding court. McAndrew had only a second or two to contemplate this scene, before a group of men came through the doors right behind him and, brushing past without even looking at the young man, started moving across the bar-room towards Harper and his companions.

Jack was not the only interested observer in the unfolding drama that evening. Standing at the bar, sipping their drinks thoughtfully, were the two newspapermen who had lately interviewed Sheriff Williams about the fate of their late colleague. They had spotted Clarence Harper and his cronies and followed them into the saloon, with no other idea than watching for a while the man who was the object of their attentions. They nearly dropped their drinks when they saw Mort Williams march in with three men, all of them quite clearly prepared for trouble. This was news all right and they were right there while it was being made!

One of the men sitting drinking with Harper said, 'Boss, I think we got company.'

Harper turned round to see what the man meant and was surprised, and more than a little displeased, to find that the hick sheriff who had been straightened out by Abe Goldman some little while back, was standing behind him with a rifle, the barrel of which was damned near poking him in the back of his neck. Nevertheless, Clarence Harper was not a man to be harsh with inferiors, unless it was strictly necessary. He said, 'Sheriff Williams. What might we do for you?'

'I'm a lookin' for two of your men, Mr Harper. One of 'em's called Rutledge. Don Rutledge. The other's name is Goldman. I don't see 'em here. Mind telling me where I can find 'em?'

'May I enquire the nature of your business with them?'

Because he was now backed up by his deputies and was being observed by them, Williams thought that he ought to put on a bit of a show and demonstrate that he was in charge, not this slick fellow from back East. Sheriff Williams said, 'You may *enquire* all you like, but I ain't about to tell you. This here's a law matter. Those men are wanted. Where are they?'

Clarence Harper stared for a moment at the rube who was now putting on side because he had an audience. Softly, Harper said, 'Sheriff, I thought you and me understood each other. I'm grieved to find that

147

you are aiming to bluster and bully me. It won't answer and you know as well as I, just precisely why that is. Now, if you'll allow me and my friends to continue our conversation in peace?' He turned back to the table.

The tension in the saloon was as tight as could be, with every pair of eyes turned to the confrontation at the back of the room. Something had to give, but what actually happened took everybody by surprise. The deputy carrying the scattergun was, in his regular life, the clerk in Sawyer's Crossing's hardware store. He was a tall, burly individual, which was why the sheriff engaged him when he was after deputies for a special occasions. He looked the part as a tough man. Charlie Baker was this man's name and, despite his imposing size, he was a nervous fellow, who was not at all given to violence. He'd been handed the sawn-off shotgun by Mort Williams and told to just hold it at his hip and look as though he wasn't afraid to use it. Before they went into the Tanglefoot, Baker had, for some unknown reason, thought it a good idea to cock the hammers of the piece he was carrying and then curl his finger round the trigger, so that he would be ready for any eventuality. The sight of those four, grim-looking men sitting with Harper was enough to make the clerk nervous and so his finger had tightened unconsciously upon the trigger.

It was typical of the slack way that Mort Williams ran his office that he didn't bother to regularly check the firearms locked up in what he was pleased to call his 'armoury', in reality, nothing more than a stout closet standing in a corner of the office, next to the fireplace. Had he ever done so, then he would have discovered that the catch holding up the hammer, once it was cocked, was worn away to almost nothing. This had given the scattergun what is sometimes known as a 'hair trigger', meaning that it was so sensitive that it might be fired by the merest brush against it. Charlie Baker found this out when he moved his weapon to get a more comfortable grip on it, but did not think to remove his finger from the trigger as he did so.

The shooting began without any of the usual preliminaries, such as name-calling, shouting and signals of aggressive intent, scarcely surprising, since nobody was really feeling angry or even mildly vexed. It was unfortunate that when Baker shifted the way in which he was holding that shotgun, he should inadvertently have fired it, the full force of the blast catching a man called Jimmy Doyle, who was one of Harper's men, in his face. At the range of no more than five feet, the blast was sufficient to send Doyle flying backwards. He was dead before he hit the sawdust-strewn floor.

The shot which killed Jimmy Doyle shocked everybody, none more so than the man who had fired it. Charlie Baker was just getting ready to frame some sort of apology, when the man who had been sitting by Doyle's side pulled his pistol and, thinking that he and the others were about to be massacred, began shooting at Mort Williams and his deputies. His first two bullets took the sheriff in the chest, before the deputy at his side had the gumption to draw and begin shooting on his own account.

For the next ten seconds, the Tanglefoot was filled with the roar of gunfire and, as the shooting continued, clouds of blue-grey smoke. The other patrons, including the journalists from the *New York Times*, had taken the precaution of flinging themselves to the floor, in order not to be cut down by some stray bullet. Jack McAndrew alone remained on his feet, staring in wonder at the extraordinary scene unfolding before his eyes. A gunfight in a bar-room was a new thing in the boy's experience, and he neither understood the conventions of such things, nor fully appreciated the danger he was in.

The shooting petered out, leaving in its wake an eerie silence. Those who had not participated in the gunfight stayed where they were until they could be perfectly sure that there was not going to be any more firing. The cloud of smoke which hung over much of the bar-room, made it hard to see what the eventual outcome of the fight had been. Then, two figures rose to their feet and walked forward towards the door. One was Clarence Harper and the other, one of his men. These two seemed to be the only survivors of the shootout which was later immortalized as the gunfight at the Tanglefoot Saloon.

CHAPTER 11

It looked as though Harper and his man were about to walk right out of the saloon after the gunfight in which the Sheriff of Sawyer's Crossing and his deputies had been killed. As they headed for the door, a slim youth stepped in front of Harper, blocking his way. What happened next was curious. The man who was walking along next to Harper didn't even break step, but just kept right on walking. He pulled back the batwings and left the saloon without stopping. He was never found, although the fellow running the livery stable vouchsafed later that the man had seemed to be in the devil of a hurry to saddle up and leave town. It was surmised that having helped kill a number of peace officers, this man was hoping to save his neck and didn't want to be delayed in his departure for anything. Perhaps he'd figured out by that time, that his job with Clarence Harper had probably ended anyway and there was no point in hazarding his life further on behalf of the Rocky

Mountains Railroad Company.

'You!' said Harper, and there was a note of resignation in his voice. 'I thought we'd meet again. What will you have now?'

The young man standing front of him and blocking his exit from the saloon, had a pistol tucked casually in his belt. For his own part, Harper appeared to be unarmed. He said, 'I'm guessing you're not the type to shoot down an unarmed man, no matter what cause you might think you have to wish him dead.'

'I wouldn't be too sure 'bout that,' said McAndrew, moving his jacket to one side with his wrist to show the Colt Navy there, ready and waiting. His hand hovered above the hilt of the pistol as though about to snatch it up at the slightest provocation.

The two of them stood like that for a space, as if they were posing for a tableau or something. Then Clarence Harper did something quite unexpected. In his younger days, Harper had made his first money working as a riverboat gambler on the Mississippi. In those days, he had fallen into the habit of concealing a muff pistol in his vest pocket. It appeared he was quite unarmed, but, when things got rough, as they invariably did from time to time, he was not altogether helpless. Over the years, Harper had bought newer models and made sure that even when he was famed as a railroad magnate, he still had a secret edge if things should ever turn nasty. He currently carried a .41 Remington derringer of a type which had only come onto the market that very year. It was a twin-barrelled version.

The truth was, Jack had not the least intention of shooting Harper, now it had come to the point. He moved his hand away from the pistol in his belt and was astounded when Harper's own right hand flicked against his chest and emerged with a tiny, shiny, nickel-plated weapon. He wasted no time, but cocked it with his thumb and pulled the trigger immediately. The young man at whom the pistol was aimed, flinched instinctively, but instead of the crash of gunfire, there came only a muffled click; signifying that the first barrel had misfired.

There came a thunderous roar and McAndrew assumed that he was as good as dead, because the gun in Clarence Harper's hand had been pointing straight at him. Oddly, he was not aware of the impact of a bullet and it was Harper who now keeled over, rather than he himself. This was puzzling in the extreme, until he turned to his left and saw that the barkeep had in his hand a .45, which he kept stowed under the bar for situations like this. The gunfight had been a confused and brief affair and although the fellow behind the bar had reached down for the gun he kept there, it seemed to him that there was no point in inviting others to shoot him, leastways not until he'd worked out which side he was on. This present case was a horse of a different colour though: a man aiming a gun at somebody with the evident intention of killing him. Under such circumstances, it was surely justifiable to open fire to prevent murder being committed right in front of his eyes.

The shot fired by the old barkeep was the last one that evening. Six men had died in the gun battle between Harper's men and Sheriff Williams and his boys. Clarence Harper's death brought the tally to seven. There had never been anything like it before in Sawyer's Crossing. Indeed, the gunfight that evening achieved nationwide fame and became almost instantly mythologized. This was due, of course, to the presence at the event of the two newspaper reporters from New York, who had witnessed the whole thing. Even before the echoes of the gunfire had died away, both men had independently come up with 'The Gunfight at the Tanglefoot Saloon' as being a catchy way to describe the confused and bloody sequence of murders which had taken place in front of their very eyes. The fact that one of those who had died was about to be come a wanted man for his part in the greatest financial swindle in the history of the United States, was the final touch which ensured that the shootout would go down in the history of the West.

After it was all over, Jack McAndrew stayed in the saloon for a time. He had been shocked by what he had witnessed and also not a little shaken by how narrowly he had himself avoided sharing the fate of those seven men. Had it not been for the misfire on Harper's muff pistol, he would have been carried out feet first himself when they were tidying up the place after the gunfight.

The two journalists had seen the youth stop Harper from leaving and saw that there was a story behind that as well. They approached McAndrew and introduced themselves to him.

'Couldn't help noticing that you didn't look like you wanted Clarence Harper to leave after all that shooting,' said the older of the two men. 'Damned near got yourself killed for it, too. You had some reason to interfere?'

McAndrew shrugged. 'I had words with the man before.'

'Mind telling us what it was about? You could get your name in the newspaper. Might even be able to offer you a fee for the interview.'

The youngster thought this proposal over for a bit and then said, 'I reckon it was a personal matter between me and Mr Harper. He's dead now, so it don't much signify.'

'Why, son,' said the other reporter, 'that's crazy! Folk'll be reading about what took place here tonight. Don't you want to be a part of it?'

'No,' said Jack McAndrew, 'I don't reckon as I do. Now if you gentlemen'll excuse me, I got business to attend to.'

The older man offered McAndrew a printed visiting card, saying, 'Here, you might as well take this, just in case you change your mind. It has my telegraphic address on as well.'

'I ain't going to change my mind,' said Jack, declining the card. 'I'm grateful to you for your attention, but I really got to make tracks now.'

After he'd gone, one of the *New York Times* men remarked to the other, 'You'd have thought that a young country boy like that would have jumped at the chance to have his name in the newspaper. I'll warrant there's a story there, you know. It's a crying shame that he wouldn't play ball with us.'

The sun was almost ready to dip below the horizon when Jack McAndrew set off back to his home. There was little point in hurrying the old mare along, because he'd not get back before the moon had risen, no matter what speed he made now. The track was a good one and led all the way back to his fields. Even in the pitch dark, the chance of the horse breaking a leg was negligible.

There were still things to clear up, but by and large, everything could hardly have worked out better. Without knowing much about the ways of railroads, it looked to him as though the line would now end at Sawyer's Crossing, which was fine. He'd no objection to that in the least. Unless an even more villainous man took over the reins of the Rocky Mountains Railroad Company, there would most likely be no further attempts to drive through the valley. So that was settled.

He wondered idly how he would explain to his mother about the fact that half the cliffs on the way to Sawyer's Crossing had collapsed. It was probably not the smart move to tell her just how they had come tumbling down; she'd have a blue fit. At some point, he'd report that there were a bunch of dead men under the rocks, maybe when a new sheriff was appointed to the town. Other than that, he'd have to start thinking more seriously about his responsibilities, now that he was the man of the place. It was time to make an end to his childhood and begin acting like a real man. That was something else that had been playing on his mind since his mother had gone away; the whole business of being a man.

When he was a kid, well, until a couple of years back really, his idea of a man was some tough fellow who could lick anybody who crossed his path. A man could shoot straight, was fearless and didn't let other folk shove him around. But since the business with the railroad had begun, McAndrew had observed that people like Clarence Harper and his henchmen were just like that. They shot people, didn't let others push them around and did much as they pleased. But was that how he wanted to end up? The young man didn't think so for a moment. There was more to being a man than not letting others shove you around and being ready, willing and able to kill men who crossed you. Any fool could do those things.

As he rode along, he thought about his father and grandfather. Sure, they had probably not been ones for letting others crowd them or dictate their actions, but there was more to them than that. They had created a farm, built a house, erected barns, raised families. Being strong and independent was important, but it wasn't all there was to being a man, that was for sure. In future, every time he found himself thinking that way, he'd try and think of the men who'd killed his brother Tom. If that was *all* you were, why you weren't much of a man at all.

The next day, Jack set off in the wagon for Fort Benton. He hoped that the rest would have done his mother good and that she might have recovered somewhat from her bereavement. Driving in that wagon surely was a slow business and, as he'd fully expected, he didn't reach the town until evening. His aunt lived on the outskirts of the settlement and she and his mother were pottering about in the vegetable garden when he drove up. Both women saw him at once and hailed him enthusiastically.

'Jack McAndrew,' said his ma, 'I declare your appearance is a perfect disgrace. See now, Izzie, how a man gets when he's no womenfolk around to tend to him? High time I was coming home!'

'Ma, you're shaming me!' he protested, but secretly the boy rejoiced. This was how his mother should be. He did not fail to mark too that this was the first time in his life that his mother had ever referred to him as a man.

Aunt Izzie said, 'Well, what's the news on this blessed railroad? It still coming by this here town?'

'Wouldn't have said so, Aunt. No, I don't think you'll be troubled by no railroad, leastways, not for a good long spell.'

'How's that, son?' asked his mother. 'That fellow change his mind?'

'I kind o' reasoned with him, Ma. You'll hear maybe a lot of foolishness talked about what has chanced since you came up here, but don't you take any heed of it.'

His mother looked at Jack sharply, the way she was apt to do when he was a little boy and she suspected that he'd been raiding the cookie jar. 'Lord,' she said, 'but you sound like your pa. Anybody get hurt while you're doing all this "reasoning"?'

He nodded. He said, 'You want to hear the details, Ma? I can tell you the men as killed our Tom are dead. That railroad boss too, if it comes to it.'

'Saints preserve us,' said Aunt Izzie. 'Sounds to me like you need to get back home soon as can be, Jenny. The boy's running loco, mark what I say.'

Despite his aunt's censorious words, the boy could not help noticing that neither she nor his mother were looking at him as though they were vexed. Quite the contrary; they both had a look in their eyes as though they were very proud of him. More, they were not looking at him as though he were a wilful child, but rather as though he were a man who needed a little steadying, feminine influence.

It was from that time onwards that Jack found that

his relationship with his mother underwent a subtle but radical change. Hitherto, he had deferred to her, offering advice but expecting her to make the final decision. When she came home, the boot was on the other foot, with his mother advising and leaving the final say to Jack, as befitted the man of the house.

His mother's grief had certainly not passed by the time that Jack brought her home from Fort Benton; it wouldn't have been in reason to have expected such a thing, but she was no longer distracted with it and was becoming more like her old self. Tom's death was not the first loss she had sustained in her life and she had always managed to surmount every such tragedy after a while.

Something which Jack noted was that even after his mother had been back for months and had had ample opportunity to hear from the Jeffersons and others about the gunfight in the Tanglefoot and the mysterious rock fall, she never once asked him a single question about any of it. She was content to know that the men who murdered her elder son were dead and that his young brother had probably had a hand in their deaths.

And that, as far as Jack McAndrew was concerned, was the end of the business. McAndrew himself never talked of the night of the gunfight and, if the subject came up while he was about, he would dismiss it, saying, 'There's a lot of nonsense talked about them days. . . .'